THE CASE OF THE SCARLET WOMAN

SHERLOCK HOLMES AND THE OCCULT

by Watkin Jones

GREENWICH EXCHANGE
LONDON

Greenwich Exchange

© Watkin Jones 1999
All rights reserved
Sir Arthur Conan Doyle characters:
Copyright © 1996 The Sir Arthur Conan Doyle Copyright holders.
Reprinted by kind permission of Jonathon Clowes Ltd. London, on behalf of
Andrea Plunket, Administrator of the Sir Arthur Conan Doyle Copyrights.

Printed and bound by Quorn Selective Repro Ltd, Loughborough
Tel: 01509 213456
Typesetting and layout by Albion Associates, London
Tel: 0208 852 4646

Greenwich Exchange Website: www.greenex.co.uk

ISBN 1 871551 14 5

In Memory of Thomas W. Jones

Watkin Jones has made in-depth study into occult theory and is a life-long enthusiast of Sherlock Holmes.

Book III: London's East End - The site of the mysteries.

CONTENTS

Preface

BOOK I: THE HAUNTED HOUSE   10

BOOK II: THE HIDDEN CHURCH   26

BOOK III: THE SCARLET WOMAN   64

PREFACE

The name, Sherlock Holmes, is surely as famous now as it ever was when he was alive. I have had some little part in this, by chronicling the various escapades that can now safely be told without fear of reprisals upon the man himself. Life has not been the same since his departure. I am not the only one who feels the loss but, whereas the public are not in possession of the one man who allowed them to sleep easy in their beds for so many years, I am the one who feels a personal loss that, I fancy, can never be made good.

I have saved long enough to purchase the flat in which, I now realise, I spent the happiest years of my life. Mrs Hudson is still here, though she is more a reminder of past times than an effective employee for age has, as with me, crept up and spread its long bony fingers firmly around our hearts.

I often look into the corner and think about trying to finish Sherlock Holmes's last chemical analysis. His apparatus remains set up as he left it in the study of his house on the Sussex Downs. The temptation of cantering and filtering the opaquely blue liquid from the conical flask under the suspended pipette is only defeated by the knowledge I would not be able to reach a result worthy of the man who started the process.

I have at last taken the advice of my own practitioner and removed the bust of Sherlock Holmes from the chair he had made his own. Those familiar with my accounts will remind themselves that Holmes himself had this bust made to entrap the vicious criminal, Colonel Sebastian Moran. Though the bullet meant for my long time friend damaged the forehead of the wax bust, I sent it back to its creator, Monsieur Oscar Meunier of Grenoble, where he set to restore it to its former glory. On its return, I placed it in the chair, slightly away from the fire, lest it should melt, and draped one of Holmes's old cloaks around it. When my own practitioner saw this he remarked that, being constantly reminded of my old friend in this way would play havoc with my nerves and so, on his advice, I had it removed and placed under an old blanket in the corner of the room. I must confess, however, that when I chance upon a queer case of criminality, I creep to the corner and give the facts of the case to this representation of Sherlock Holmes.

I have, at times, despaired at the injustice of outliving my old friend these last few years and feel somewhat saddened at having to redress one of the major omissions from my previous accounts of his singular nature. However, it would not do him justice if the occasions, of which there were markedly few, where he failed to reach the bottom of a case, were not recorded. I think Holmes would admit that, despite his exasperation, he often learned more from these experiences and so was able to bring many of the most evil men and women to justice.

The case, or at least, collection of three intertwined incidents, that I recount here are the most perfect example of Holmes being able to turn foil to his own advantage.

I shall be long gone by the time this collection is made public, if, that is, it ever will be. But before I may be accused of cowardice I would be obliged if the reader allows me the chance to explain the long secrecy. Perhaps, with the benefit of hindsight, you will understand when I tell you that there are some things that are beyond the realms of mortal man. At times, The Case Of The Scarlet Woman would be well placed in this unique categorisation and I should only want the intimate details to be known when I myself have a better understanding. I fear this will only come when I tread with angels or their diabolical equivalent. Both myself and Holmes remained taciturn on the subject of this case and even now, in my twilight years, I question the pertinence of elucidating the details contained herein.

JOHN H. WATSON, M.D.

BOOK I

THE HAUNTED HOUSE

CHAPTER ONE
A Chance Meeting

Colonel Pemberton was of that disposition that is all too rare in the ranks of to-day's officers, for he never took too lightly the considerable advantage he had over those of a less privileged class. As such, those soldiers under his command could expect a fairness of treatment not prevalent in most regiments. He was a man to be respected by sergeant majors and gunners alike, though this respect was not gained through the harsh discipline that most young soldiers experience but, rather, through a finer appreciation of each man's virtue. It was a pleasure, as much as a war would allow, to be under the command of Colonel Pemberton in the Afghanistan campaign.

Although the Colonel's hair had receded slightly in the five years since I had seen him last, he was still a fine figure of a man, standing well over six foot. Perhaps the reader would expect one of our great men of honour – for that afternoon he was to receive his knighthood – to dine only in such establishments as Simpson's or the Savoy. But he had offered to meet me in the Cheshire Cheese public house, set back from Fleet Street. I should not have concerned myself – for he was as at home in the Cheshire Cheese as much as he was in grander places. It was with great sadness that I bid him a fond farewell when he made haste towards the Palace.

I also had a full afternoon, having to catch a recital of Mozart's Sonata in A that was to take place in Queen's Street. I had a seat forced upon me by one of my more illustrious patients, as a mark of his appreciation following recovery from a rather severe case of influenza. It is hard to refuse such an offering from a gentleman so used to having his own way and, although the particular piece in question was slightly too fast for my own taste, I had been reliably informed that the tickets were much sought after in the higher reaches of society.

As more and more people left the bar room for their afternoon's work, the smoke seemed to thin out slightly as the crisp autumn air worked its way in from the courtyard. I relished the last drops of brandy, collected my coat and hat and made towards the door. No sooner had I took hold of the handle, however, did I hear a familiar voice.

"Ah, Watson! What is your business here?"

I spun around in the direction from where the voice had come and saw a shadowy figure sitting at a small table in the corner, next to the window. The features were not discernible, for the light was temporarily in my eyes, but the outline of that famous face was unmistakable. The long chin, the thin cheeks and the slightly hooked nose were as well known to me as if they were my own. It was the world's greatest consulting detective, and my old friend, Mr Sherlock Holmes.

"Why, Holmes, I left you a message two weeks ago, but got no reply," I said.

"Alas, Watson, I have been away. Indeed the only reason I am in this area today is in the course of a most queer case that has drawn me from the fresh Sussex countryside where I have been indulging in my new interest of bee-keeping. If you would be so good as to join me, I am sure that your chronicles would benefit considerably from the strange events that have assailed my client so."

"Well, I do have an appointment, Holmes," I replied.

"And one you are not so sure of keeping."

"Well, I suppose a quick glass of beer will not be too much," I conceded.

Holmes returned from the bar with two glasses of ale and immediately set about stuffing his pipe with that rough, pungent shag, the smell of which was a constant reminder of our days together in the apartment at 221B Baker Street. All the time he held the pipe in his hands, he did not take his eyes from my face. His stare finally broke when he offered me some of the tobacco, which I gratefully received, having given my last ounce to Colonel Pemberton.

Holmes leant back in the chair, with his pipe close to his lips and said, "So you have been thinking about Afghanistan, Watson?"

"How the devil did you know that? But of course, you saw me lunching with Colonel Pemberton and recalled his visit to our apartment some years ago."

"I have only just arrived, Watson, and I did not spy either one of you until I saw you making to leave, though I am most unfortunate in having missed the dear Colonel, a most agreeable friend of yours."

"Then how did you know I have been talking about Afghanistan?"

"Mere observation. It is evident that you have loosened your shirt slightly and rubbed a finger on the inside of the collar. A slight reddening of the skin is quite clear even in this light. It is a habit of yours I have observed whenever you recall your time in the Campaign. No doubt it derives from your time as a somewhat heavily dressed officer loosening his clothes against the intense heat of summer in Afghanistan."

"Ah, your observation is as acute as ever, Holmes. But please do proceed with the details of your new case."

"Well, you have caught me at the best of times, Watson, for my investigation has not yet begun. I shall be brief as to what has passed, as way of formulating a case that is queer in the extreme, and then perhaps you would be so good as to give me your valued views.

"As I have already explained, I was taking some time away in pursuit of my new interest, when I received a visit from a young man by the name of John Williams. Quite a lively man he is too. It was no surprise to find that he works as an estate agent. Anyway, his troubles were enough to compel him to seek me out and visit me as far away as the Sussex Downs. On hearing his tale, I agreed to take on the case as it will surely prove most singular. I have arranged to meet him here. He should arrive in twenty minutes, which leaves me with enough time to give you the bare facts.

"The basic fact of the case is that young Mr Williams has had some difficulty in selling one of his properties and the reason he gives, or has been led to believe, is that the house is haunted. At the beginning of each year, Mr Williams's employer tells him the number of houses to be sold by the time the year draws to an end. With only nine months gone, he has already equalled the target that will see him promoted in the company, aside, that is, from this one house. The property in question is in Chancery Lane and has been on the market for three months. I am led to believe that it is a most favourable location and there should be little difficulty in disposing of it.

"What Mr Williams has had to endure over the last three months is hardly believable and, indeed, lesser men than you or I would surely suggest the occurrence of supernatural phenomena. For, no sooner does Mr Williams show prospective clients in to the first floor rooms of the house then they turn on their heels and flee, for no apparent reason, some he says, actually screamed."

"So, Mr Williams has come to the conclusion that the house is haunted?"

"He is a rational man, Watson, and as such, is at pains not to believe in the existence of a haunted house, but I fear he is at the end of his wits and has called upon me as a last resort. But this is not all, for the most singular point is yet to be explained."

"And what might that be, Holmes?"

"On his last visit to the house, at some time towards the end of last week, Mr Williams showed a couple the premises and, after they too had run distraught from the property, he found himself alone. He was descending the stairs, somewhat despondent at yet another potential sale ruined, when he heard a noise, turned and saw a piece of wood being hurled through the air directly towards his head. It was as much as he could do to avoid the projectile before it clattered against the door and fell to the floor."

"Then there was an attempted assault on him, Holmes, and this incident goes to prove that the house is not haunted but there is a criminal explanation."

"This is the singular point that makes the case so interesting. Mr Williams did not see anybody hurl the wood at him and he believes that the object appeared out of thin air."

"Surely, he has come to that conclusion because of the shock? Pieces of wood do not appear from nowhere."

"As I would say myself," replied Holmes. I felt flattered. He continued, "I am to visit the house this afternoon to investigate the claims, though I already have a certain hypothesis as to where the investigation might lead us."

"I have no hypothesis whatsoever Holmes, at least not from the evidence you have given."

"Well, there is one important fact that I have not told you. Young Mr Williams is in love and engaged to a young lady, and I am assured that his feelings are reciprocated. Mr Williams did not volunteer this information, and it was not until I prompted him, having seen the slight rouge stain on his shirt, that he admitted to having a fiancée. Aside from the young couple, we are the only ones who know about the affair, for both parties are certain that should the lady's father find out, he would break off the engagement at once. This is particularly important, since the young lady is none other than Annabel Grunston, the daughter of his employer, Mr Grunston of Grunston Associates."

"Then this Mr Grunston has found out about his daughter's relationship with Mr Williams."

"That is indeed my tentative conclusion. To some extent, this explanation is supported by the odd coincidence of Grunston offering an incentive to sell the property. I have already made some enquiries, have been quite assured that it is not normal practice to offer incentives in such a way."

Holmes relit the pipe that had been extinguished in the length of time it had taken him to retell the facts. He fell silent and lost himself in thought. I told him about the concert that I was due to attend that afternoon.

"But, Watson, this is a most unique case and one that I would not miss for the world. Surely it would be better to fill up your diaries with these events than to listen to Mozart's Sonata, even I have always found it too detached a piece, too morbid to begin and too fast to end," replied Holmes.

"Yes, you are right, Holmes. But if it is all the same, I should send a telegram, offering some explanation."

"Indeed, Watson, tell them you are at the mercy of your profession and that you must attend to a gravely ill patient."

I was only away for ten minutes and when I returned to the public house, Holmes had replenished both our glasses and was sat in solitude.

"Quick Watson, sit down! I do believe our client has just come through the door," he ordered as I approached.

I did as he said and followed the direction of his stare. In the doorway, casting his eyes around the room, was a young man. He was of smallish height and a few years before thirty. He had drawn, thin brows and a thin face, which had reddened slightly from the walk he had obviously just made. He turned and recognised Holmes, straightened his jacket and showed a full set of teeth in a good humoured smile. He walked quickly towards us and sat at the extra chair before being asked. He was nervous in the extreme and his smile, I realised, was merely a consequence of his nervousness.

"Mr Holmes, it is so good of you to come," he said, rubbing his hands under the table.

"Not at all my good fellow, a case that promises to be as singular as yours is a most attractive proposition. But I must introduce you to my trusted friend and colleague, Dr Watson. He has considerable experience in supporting me with my various investigations and is most trustworthy. Anything you wish to say to me, can be said in his presence."

"But of course," replied Mr Williams, turning to me and stretching his hand out in greeting, "It is a pleasure to meet you, Dr Watson. I have read all your articles. You are indeed a remarkable man." I felt quite touched by the sincerity with which he spoke.

"Tell me, Mr Williams, how are you finding your new bicycle?" said Holmes suddenly.

The man turned quickly to face Holmes, who was smiling slightly. "How do you know I have a new bicycle?"

"You have a new pair of trousers, my dear sir, and yet there is a slight mark on the inside right ankle. The mark can only be due to your leg rubbing against a bicycle chain and, as your trousers are so new, I would suggest that you had not realised the necessity of a pair of clips."

"Absolutely astounding!" cried the man.

"Mere observation. To discuss the business we have, I have explained the facts to my colleague as you have given them to me, Mr Williams," continued Holmes quickly, "Though we would be much obliged if you could give us any other information that you may have remembered since our last meeting."

The man's complexion suddenly took on a much paler shade. "I have nothing more for you, Mr Holmes. I have not been able to return to that horrible house, and fear that my nerves will not be able to take much more. I implore that you should come to some speedy resolution, for my sanity depends on it, of that I am sure. It is most horrible, most diabolical."

"Then we shall lose no time in making our way to Chancery Lane, and to the property that has played on your mind in such an adverse way," said Holmes calmly, laying a hand on the man's arm.

CHAPTER TWO
The Haunted House

The evening was drawing in by the time the three of us made our way along Fleet Street and turned into Chancery Lane. Williams led the way at a pace Holmes had little difficulty in keeping up with, but one which I found exhausting. As we neared the property that was to be the beginning of our enquiries, Williams shortened his strides and began to hang back. Holmes, on sensing this, took the lead, dodging quickly between parked hansom cabs waiting for fares outside the Inner Temple. Holmes stopped outside the house in question. I passed our client, who had stopped short and was looking up at the first floor windows with a growing foreboding of the place.

"Is this the property?" asked Holmes in a crisp manner.

"Yes, Mr Holmes, and if you do not mind, I think that I will stay out here while you have a look. Here's the key."

Holmes took the key that was offered him and walked quickly to the door. I followed and entered after Holmes had struggled with the ill-fitting key. The door had hardly room to close in the small space in which we found ourselves. A bare wooden staircase rose up in front of us but, as I made for the first step, I was held back by Holmes. He spent some time tapping the two walls to either side. The door slammed shut under the force of a fierce gust of wind. He took his glass out to study the back of the door.

"Halloa!" he cried suddenly, "Here is the mark that corresponds to a heavy object striking the door. You notice how the paint has chipped away cleanly, and the edge of the break has no dust."

I listened to what he said, hoping for an explanation, but in vain, for Holmes had begun to climb the side of the stairway. "Make sure you follow exactly in my footsteps, Watson, so your heavy boots do not obscure the already smudged marks."

Holmes walked on in silence, occasionally looking behind to make sure I was following his instructions. On every other step, he would stop and examine the two steps in front of him. When he turned to me half way up, his face was grave:

"It is as I feared, Watson, any traces that may have been left by the perpetrator of this extraordinary incident have been destroyed. Too many people have been up and down these stairs. However, there is one distinguishing feature. Do you see some of the more prominent foot marks?" I looked down, followed Holmes's outstretched finger and saw faint outlines of greasy dust. "They are, no doubt, marks left by the more heavy of Mr Williams's clients. Now, here we have a large gentleman with worn, square toed boots. It is evident that they are worn from the crack in the flat of the right boot. Here we can see the way he came in, as the toe is pointing forwards; but notice the same boot in the opposite direction. There is a large imprint of the front of the sole, with hardly any marking of the split. He has also missed some of the steps, which suggests that he was running down the stairs on his way out. Alas, this tells us little aside from the fact that young Williams has been telling us the truth thus far."

On reaching the top of the stairs, we found ourselves in a small corridor with two doors closed to our right. The first led into a large, bare room with a pungent musty smell. The bay windows let little light in as they were covered with heavy black curtains, and the floor had several loose boards that creaked as we both walked towards the windows and drew back the curtains. Holmes stood by the window for some five minutes, scanning the exterior surroundings. From over his shoulder, I could see our client waiting beneath a gas lamp on the other side of the street, looking furtively from side to side, as if under some sort of threat.

Holmes pushed the window open, leaned out and shouted across the street. "Mr Williams, I assure you that there is no danger here at the moment, so I would very much like you to come on up and answer some questions I have to put to you."

As soon as Holmes was sure that Williams was coming, he bounded across the room and out to the top of the stairs. I heard the door slam close from beneath and immediately felt a strong wind rush through the room. I closed the window to keep the chill out, before turning to greet our client. Williams had turned pale and stopped dead at the doorway. "It is quite alright, Mr Williams, there is nothing to fear," said Holmes calmly.

"But surely you felt the wind, Mr Holmes," stuttered the nervous Williams.

"Merely a difference in pressure between the open window and the front door. By holding a small square of tissue paper aloft, I detected that the wind rushed from the window, down the stairs to the door. That is nature's way; from the high pressure to the low. Nothing ghostly, I assure you.

"Although I did use your entrance as a test, I should like to ask you some questions. How long has the property been vacant?"

"Since April, four months at most."

"Have the curtains been drawn all that time?"

"No, I had them drawn for my last client, he wished to have a closer look at the material. Unfortunately, as with those that preceded him, he ran out of the house screaming soon after touching the material. It was at that time that the piece of wood was hurled at me. I have not been back since."

"Ah yes, the wood. I presume this is the piece?" said Holmes, pointing to a small plank of timber on the floor behind the door.

"Yes, I think that is the one. Yes, I am sure it is the same," murmured the man, looking aghast at the object.

"And nobody has been in the house since then?" continued Holmes as he bent to pick up the object.

"No, nobody."

"Who else has keys to the house?"

"There are two sets – I have one and there is a spare set that are kept in the safe in the office."

"Does Mr Grunston have access to the safe in the office?"

"Yes, he has the only set of keys to the safe. If I require anything, he insists that he should be the one to open the safe. Here, do you really think that he has something to do with this?"

"There are many theories, my occupation is to find the only one that fits all the facts. What about the previous tenant? Does he have a set of keys?"

"He returned the keys when he moved out."

"But he could have made a copy, could he not?"

"It would not have done any good, Mr Holmes, for I have seen to it that the locks have been changed. Every property has the locks changed once a tenant vacates."

Holmes remained silent for several minutes, turning the piece of wood over and over in his hands, studying each grain in great detail. Suddenly, he threw the wood at the wall with an immense force, whereupon it split clean in two and fell to the floor. Williams and I jumped, but Holmes returned to his state of melancholic thought, picking up the two pieces and inspecting them carefully. He walked out of the room and I could hear his footsteps descend the stairs. After some time, he returned and began to work his way around the room, taking his glass out to examine the floor at either end. Once he had made this thorough examination of the floor, he returned to the curtains and scrutinised them for some time.

When his examination was complete, he turned to us with bright, alert eyes. "Well, Watson, I think that our work here is complete. If we hurry, we will be in time to catch one of Mrs Hudson's handsome dinners at Baker Street, where we can think about the evidence that has presented itself this afternoon. There is a fair amount of promise in this case and I feel that it will certainly stretch us to our logical limits. If there are any new developments, Mr Williams, I would thank you to inform me immediately. In the mean time, we shall leave you to lock up and bid you a good evening. Come along, Watson." With his parting comment, Holmes took me firmly by the arm and dragged me from the house.

Once outside, he urged me across the street and into a small alley, whereupon he pushed me against the wall. I looked into the darkness we had entered; the alley extended for some way before flowing into a picturesque square known as Bishop Court. Holmes put a finger to my lips and kept an arm up against me to make sure I did not stray from the wall. He leaned around the entrance to the alley but pulled back when he saw Williams leave the house and walk at a fast pace towards Holborn. From some distance, it was still possible to see the grief and disappointment on the man's face.

When Williams had disappeared from sight, Holmes turned to me, straightening out my jacket lapels that had creased under his rough treatment. "I think it is necessary that we do some detection work in the absence of our client, Watson. If you are up to it, I should once again ask you to step onto the wrong side of the law, though you can be assured that we are strongly on the side of morality."

Visions of our escapade on Hampstead Heath in the pursuit of the evil criminal, Charles Milverton, came back to haunt me but Holmes was already out of the alley and heading towards the house. I had caught him by the time he had reached the front door, only to find him despondent. "Look here, Watson, it is a most complex lock. I would not be able to pick this without drawing suspicion to ourselves, but it is most singular that the estate agent should wish to fit such an expensive lock to what can only be described as a modest dwelling."

"A modest dwelling it may well be, Holmes, but I do not care to loiter about here for too long. I would be much obliged if we could start as quickly as possible, so as not to be bait for some of the less desirable specimens that frequent this district after dark."

"You are quite right, Watson. It is not the time to dwell on my findings thus far; we must secure our entrance, whereupon we will have the rest of the night to think about the case."

"The rest of the night, Holmes? But surely..." My protest fell on deaf ears as my companion was already on his way to the small, deserted alley that flanked the house. Holmes stopped next to a discarded box and turned it on its end. "If you could keep a sentry on the road, Watson, then once I am in, I will let you through the front door."

As I walked back to Chancery Lane, I could hear the window being forced open behind me and Holmes making his illicit entrance. A couple of minutes later, the latch on the door was lifted and Holmes ushered me in quickly. The large first floor room was almost in darkness, as the light outside faded and the half drawn curtains blocked most of the sun's dying rays.

I was left on my own in the room for the best part of half an hour, while I could hear Holmes moving on the opposite side of the wall. He returned with a candle, cradling the flame in a cupped hand. "I believe my suspicions to be correct in as much as the clues to our mystery lie firmly in this room. Make yourself comfortable, Watson, I fear that it could be a long night."

Holmes closed the curtains and settled himself on the floor with the candle stuck in a small bulb of melted wax he had poured onto a wooden floorboard. I lowered myself until I was sat on the floor with my back against the wall. "I shall wake you if anything untoward should happen, Watson. If you would be as good as to hand me your revolver then you can settle down; there is no point in both of us losing out on a night's sleep."

"I shall do nothing of the sort, Holmes. You may have the gun but I assure you I will not be able to catch my night's sleep in this fashion."

Holmes sat in silence, the candle flickering shadows across his long face, showing his eyes to be distant. My own eyes were beginning to droop when I heard the bells of St. Andrew's church in Holborn and Clement Danes on the Strand fighting each other to chime out two o'clock. Holmes did not flinch, his rigid body remaining perfectly still in a state of alert for any sound out of the usual.

"I fear, Watson, that we may have to put the candle out," he said eventually, "If you will allow me to have your box of matches, I should be ready to light it at a moment's warning."

The extinguishing of our only source of light was accompanied by a crisp wind whistling suddenly through the room. Once it had past, we were again left in silence. The last thing I heard was the three o'clock chimes, before drifting into a heavy slumber.

I was woken by the light streaming through the windows that were no longer covered by the heavy curtains. "Ah, good morning, Watson," said Holmes. I squinted through my tired eyes at his outline. He was pacing up and down the room, his chin in the fingers of his right hand, while his left hand held his pipe.

"Holmes! What time is it?"

"Six," he replied absently.

"Ah, then that would explain how tired I feel."

"I fear you did not sleep well, Watson. You had your fair share of nightmares by the sound of your shouts through the early hours."

"Well, now that you mention it, I did have a queer dream."

Holmes showed some considerable interest in my reply. In two bounds, he was hovering over me, his energy causing him to shift his weight from foot to foot. "Please tell me of your dream, Watson."

I really do not see that it should be of any interest, it makes little enough sense to me. I am sure those French psychologists would have a field day with my visions but, if you insist, I shall endeavour to explain what I can remember." I paused while Holmes lowered himself to the floor and turned all his attention to my story. "I had a feeling of a battle. It was surely a battle between good and evil, fought in this very room. At one end was a huge black beast, breathing fire from two nostrils, seemingly at will. At the other end stood a lowly old crone draped in a white robe, her only defence being the ability to make herself invisible when under threat of a good scorching from the flaming beast. For what seemed like hours, the two stalked each other round the room. Occasionally a little monster would appear between the two but would be quickly vaporised by either the wand of the crone or the flames of the beast.

"The duel began with a great flash of electricity from the end of a sturdy staff the crone held up to her opponent, but it was stopped short by a flame fanning out from the great beast. The flame continued and looked set to strike the crone when she became invisible, only to re-emerge behind her opponent. The beast whirled round and made to strike once more but the crone disappeared once again, reappearing in her original position. This duelling went on for some time, interspersed with various hideous spirits popping up, only to be struck dead by one of the two fighters. By the time the battle neared its end, the floor was littered by the dead spirits of the various pawns. It was like a game of chess, with only the two kings left to fight it out, neither having the ability to win. That was when the light from the windows woke me."

"You are right, Watson, the psychologists would surely have great fun with your descriptions," said Holmes when I had finished.

"But surely this can have nothing to do with our case, Holmes?"

"There has to be some explanation of the sequence of events endured by Williams and we have to consider all possible explanations until facts prove them to be false, though I am inclined to deduce that this strange atmosphere has made no small impression on your imagination," replied Holmes as he lifted himself from the floor and walked towards the window. "Quick, Watson! Come quickly," he shouted suddenly.

I rushed over to where he was standing and followed the direction of his eyes out of the window and into the alley below. Just before disappearing from sight, I could see a caped figure running away.

"We were too slow, Watson, she will be long gone now. She must have spotted me."

CHAPTER THREE
An Unsatisfactory Conclusion

I was pleased to find myself safely installed back into the apartment in Baker Street. I sat in my old armchair, thoroughly satisfied by one of Mrs Hudson's breakfasts, while Holmes sat opposite me, plucking and then drawing a bow across his violin strings. I knew that the violin was merely an aide to stimulate him, a way of shutting out any distraction that may have led him away from the immediate problem.

"Perhaps it would be prudent to let you know how far my thinking on this case has gone, Watson," he said eventually.

"I should very much like to hear your conclusions."

"Then you shall, and maybe you will see a way forward that has escaped me. I should start from the very beginning, since you only became involved after our meeting at the Cheshire Cheese. The first thing that I had to establish was whether my client's story was correct, or whether he was under the influence of some sort of delusion. I am sure you would agree with me, Watson, when I say that we have often heard of just such tales of hauntings as these, only to find them to be pure fiction on the part of the teller."

"I suppose it is necessary to test the legitimacy of the case, Holmes, but for my part I think the man to be quite genuine."

"He may well have seemed genuine, but now I can prove that his story is to be believed. You will remember that I made a careful examination of the Chancery Lane staircase, where the footmarks showed that people had been in quite a hurry to get out. There was also a mark on the door, where the timber crashed past young Williams's head, which led me to search for the piece, which was found in the upstairs room. There are some most singular details to be seen in this evidence, however. Firstly, the mark on the door was fresh, but had only dislodged a small patch of paint. If a piece of timber of that size had been thrown from the top of the stairs, I would expect to see more extensive damage to the woodwork. Secondly, the piece of timber hardly had a mark on it. I threw it at the wall upstairs with the same force as would have been needed to reach the door from the top of the stairs. The wood split down the middle, as expected. It is a queer point indeed that the wood should not have split when it was hurled at our client."

"Yes, Holmes, but surely if the wood impacted lengthways, the force would not be enough to split."

"Ah, and that was my first thought, however, there was a slight mark on the end of the timber that would correspond to the collision with the door."

"You assume Mr Williams's story to be false then?"

"Not at all, Watson. It was patently obvious that the man was scared out of his wits. It is rare indeed that a fraudster can fake such foreboding and outright fear of a place as Williams has of that house. The wood was thrown, though it must have somehow floated rather than travel at the speed I would expect. Now, I shall leave that thought with you and begin to explain what I found in the apartment. You may have noticed the interest I took in the floor of that room and I do believe that even you noticed the remarkable indentations at either end of the room. Well, it was possible to deduce not merely the obvious that there were two large objects placed at either end of the room at one time, but that one of them was coloured white and the other black. It was easy to detect the small flakes of coloured varnish in the two sets of grooves.

"The difference in colour has a significance that is not at first apparent, but is more obvious if you take into account the traces of blood on the floor where the black furniture had been placed. I had expected to find them."

"But why did you expect to find blood?"

"It will all fall into place if you follow my reasoning, but firstly I must tell you about the curtains, they were a feat, even for me. The first thing to note was that the sun had bleached the underside of them considerably, which led me to deduce they had been drawn for some time. That, in itself, is suggestive of a peculiar activity. It could be that the previous tenant did not want to be seen from the outside, but this is an unnecessary precaution, for there is no point from where a man outside could see into the room. So the only alternative is that the activity inside the room needed to be away from sunlight. But there is yet another point to be made on the curtains and that is the smell that lingered on the rough material. It was not something familiar to me, though definitely herbal. It was not unlike the pungent aroma of opium, yet it had the sweeter scent of jasmine. Surely it was an incense of some kind that had lingered for these last few months."

"But how can you say it was definitely from incense?"

"Quite elementary. If you shook the curtain, dust would fall from the inner side of the material, but not from that side closest to the window. The origin of the heavy dust particles was from inside the room."

"I do not see that this leads us any closer to the answer though, Holmes," I protested.

"Ah, but if you widen the scope of your reasoning, you should be able to come up with an activity that encompasses all the shreds of evidence thus far. The lack of sunlight, the incense, the blood and what I believe to be two altars, one white and one black, can only mean one thing: a practising occultist. It is fairly coincidental that I have just finished reading a fine monograph by A.P. Sinnett on the very same subject."

"Who do you suspect as being this occultist, then?"

"The previous tenant. I learned from Mr Williams that his name is Aleister Crowley and shortly before I happened upon you yesterday, I made some enquiries and found that, indeed, he is known as a somewhat eccentric man and believes himself to have powers that would be attributed to a witch."

"This all sounds too incredible to me, Holmes."

"You saw that shrouded woman run from the alley yesterday. Her outfit was somewhat out of the ordinary wouldn't you say?"

"Yes, I suppose you are right. But how does this explain the attack on young Williams?"

"There is still work to be done, Watson. But make no mistake, we are dealing with people who are secretive by their nature, so we have to tread carefully to find a motive for the attack."

There were plenty more questions I wished to ask Holmes, but we were interrupted by the entrance of Mrs Hudson, who promptly handed him a telegram that had just been delivered. I looked at the expression on the face of Holmes as he read through the lines. His brow seemed to tighten across his eyes and his lips thinned even more than usual. He read the message a number of times before promptly throwing it into the flames of the fire. He clasped his hands together and ran his fingertips over his lips.

"What is it, Holmes? What is wrong?" I cried.

"It is most unsatisfactory, Watson, that is what. It is a message from Williams, telling us the investigation has finished. Our services are no longer needed as he has this very morning sold the house. And it is a great pity that we were not given the opportunity to take the case to its natural, or perhaps unnatural, conclusion."

Although these were the last words Holmes had to say on the subject, the name of Aleister Crowley was to appear once again. Perhaps all the more important, the woman who we spied in the alley off Chancery Lane was to play her part in two of our most frightening cases, namely those of the Hidden Church and the Scarlet Woman.

BOOK II
THE HIDDEN CHURCH

CHAPTER ONE
A Kidnapping

It was the month of April, the fourth month of our new century and Sherlock Holmes was as much in demand as ever, despite the retirement he would talk of so often. He would spend most of his waking hours jumping from one case to another and then back again as if they were all indeterminably linked. But this was far from the reality, for he was the most remarkable man in as much as he could put one idea from his mind, detach himself completely from it whilst devoting all his attention to something else, only to return to the first idea at some future point without forgetting the smallest detail. I had moved back into Baker Street on Holmes's suggestion, from where it was only a short walk to my thriving practice, and on the morning in question, found Holmes at his desk, cutting pages from a number of separate monographs ranging from the fine teas of the colonies to new explosive techniques in armaments. I looked over his shoulder without him stirring from his reading.

"Ah! Watson, I hope my revolver practice was not too much of an inconvenience to you last night," Holmes said suddenly, looking up at me with a tired but nevertheless alert eye.

"Well, it certainly gave me a start when you began, but I dare say that it was in a worthy cause. On which case are you working at the moment? No doubt there is more than one, given the extraordinary breadth of documentation here," I replied, pointing to the pile of papers on the desk.

"No. Just the one, Watson. I have sent message to Inspector Lestrade so that he may take the necessary steps to apprehend the perpetrator of the Kensington Tea Room murder."

"Ah, so who is the perpetrator of that ghastly crime?"

"I dare say you will be able to read of it in this evening's paper, Watson, after which I should be pleased to give you a full explanation. However, until then, I must get some semblance of order back into these rooms. I fear I have let my untidy habits go a touch too far in the pursuit of justice."

For the first time that I have in memory, Sherlock Holmes proceeded to tidy his papers that were in an even more extravagant state of disarray than was normal. But it was at this point that Mrs Hudson brought us our breakfast and I was pleased to see that Holmes ate heartily.

"Not quite up to the standard of those breakfasts in the country, eh Watson?" he said.

This was true. Holmes had been immersed in case after case since he had returned from his period of rest in Sussex, where he had replenished energy and nerve. The break had not been complete, for there was the intervention of the most peculiar case in Chancery Lane, the unsatisfactory conclusion of which had not been to the advantage of Holmes's disposition. But, with a few more weeks, he was as good as new, and only too eager to return to our apartment in Baker Street and the bustle of metropolitan life.

Colour seemed to be returning to his cheeks with every bite of food. I leant back having consumed less than half of what Sherlock Holmes had already cleared and left him to finish in silence, retiring to the fire that Mrs Hudson had lit to keep away the morning chill. From past the windows I could hear the wheels of the carts rumbling over the ruts in the street below. I have to admit that the sleep I had, interrupted by Holmes's shooting during the night, was not enough to prevent me dozing.

I was woken some time later by a hasty tap on my shoulder, followed by a vigorous shake. "Watson! We have a visitor," I heard Holmes cry as I came round.

Sure enough, Mrs Hudson tapped lightly on the door and proceeded to inform us a young lady was waiting downstairs. Holmes sat in his chair, lighting the pipe that had been extinguished amid his excitement. His face was the picture of anticipation, as he leaned forward, listening to the footsteps that were audible even to my untrained ear. "Tall and slim," he whispered absently to himself.

The door opened slowly, as if the visitor was having second thoughts about her action. Finally, after what seemed like minutes and with neither one of us daring to let out the breath we had held in our lungs, a tall, slender woman entered. She was dressed almost entirely in black. Her hat had the breadth of rim that shadowed her face, and her dress, although in the more traditional cut, was freely flowing and decorated with almost insignificant black jade. It was only when she took her hat off and turned full onto us that I almost let out a cry. Her profile was nothing but beauty and there was no more than a suggestion of maquillage on her clear skinned face. Her dark eyes glittered, contrasting with the matted jade and her auburn hair shone with a life of its own. I managed to take my eyes from our visitor and turn them to Holmes who had stood into, what seemed like, a stone-like pose. I knew that he had seen what I had. She could have been a younger sister of Irene Adler. Her stature, beauty and full eyes had us both frozen in the same thoughts.

After a few uncomfortable moments, I stood up, remembering my manners, which seemed to prompt Holmes, who stretched his long frame to its full height and held a hand to our visitor.

"I have come to find Sherlock Holmes," said the woman quickly. Her accent was of that pure crystal you can only find in the north but far from being the rough diamond, it had been cut, as if by the Hatton Garden merchants themselves, into a jewel of refinement. A voice to break the strongest of characters.

That there was no hint of the American possibly jolted Holmes into action. "I am he," he replied, "but whom do I have the pleasure of addressing?"

"I am Tanith Hekaltey," she said as she stepped forward to take his outstretched hand.

"This is my friend and sometime chronicler, Dr Watson."

"Pleased to meet you, Dr Watson," she said.

"The pleasure is all mine."

"Now what is the tragedy that has plagued you this fine morning, Miss Hekaltey?" said Holmes when our guest had seated herself.

"You are the famous Sherlock Holmes, so I should know that I can keep little from you," she said after raising a finely shaped eyebrow in surprise.

"I deal only in what is self evident, Miss Hekaltey. Forgive me, your maquillage is perfect in every way, a truly wonderful subtlety, which is why I question the slight pale shade on the side of your cheek. Surely someone who has such attention to detail would notice the moisture mark that plagues many of our beautiful women. So I suggest that, as it is not raining, it was caused by a tear that escaped your handkerchief"

"Why, that is astounding, Mr Holmes," she cried, "I was not certain that I should come to you, but your powers most certainly live up to their reputation. If any person can help me with this terrible grief, then surely you are the very man."

"I am flattered by your comments, but I fear that it is only the simplest of observation," he replied, evidently pleased with her praise. "Please tell me your problem and I shall be happy to do everything to remove it from your mind."

"I am not sure that I should be seeking advice, Sir," replied the woman, slipping into a mood of sudden uncertainty, "They have warned me to be secret, else a frightful turn of events must surely proceed on their wicked course."

"Please, feel free to air the problem. Your secret is safe with both myself and Dr Watson. You must tell us the circumstance, for I sense you are in danger and that the warning is not to be treated lightly."

"You are the only hope I have, Mr Holmes. I cannot call in the police for it will result in tragedy, of that I am sure. Perhaps it would be best if I should show you what was sent to me this morning before explaining any further." Miss Hekaltey opened her bag, produced a sheet of torn foolscap and passed it to Holmes. He studied it intently for some minutes, his brows narrowing over every word before handing it to me.

Far from word being written on the sheet, the words were made from letters cut from newsprint. They were adhered along rough lines, some letters being larger than others, evidently having been taken from different publications. The letters were not what caused me to grow cold with fear though, it was the message:

WE HAVE MR HEKALTEY
GIVE NO WORD TO ONE SOLE
AND WE SHALL NOT HARM HIM
SECRECY IS ALL!!
HE HAS TO PAY.
HE BEAR'S A TRAITOR'S BRAND
A LIAR'S BRAND.

I read through the message a number of times before I heard Holmes break the eerie silence that had descended on the room. A silence the warm crackle of the fire could do nothing against.

"Is this all you have received, Miss Hekaltey? Surely they must need something from you?"

"No, this is all I received to be sure. I waited for an hour after it had fallen through the letter box to see if anything further would arrive, but there was nothing."

"Perhaps you had best give us the story, beginning with who the kidnapped person is – your father?"

"No, he is my younger brother. My father is dead and Rupert is my only sibling. He lived in a boarding house in Battersea and was hoping to become a clerk in the city. He was only in London since Saturday, four days, and I was..." The woman broke off as tears fell and she could control herself no longer. Holmes looked at me and made a sign that I should be the one to comfort her. He picked up the letter once again.

I placed my arm gently around her shoulder and felt her shaking with fear. She soon apologised for her breaking down. "Most understandable in the circumstances Miss Hekaltey, there is no need to apologise, is there Holmes?" I said.

"No. No there is no need," he said absently, looking at the paper but focusing some distance past it, in that common dreamlike state of his. "Perhaps," he said at last, "the interview would be best conducted through my questions. It is evident that your brother has been kidnapped, though for what reason we have little clue. May I ask why your brother came to London?"

Miss Hekaltey seemed to respond well to Holmes's method of extracting her story. She lifted her head and wiped away the tears with her sleeve in a way that is so characteristic of English ladies. "My father died, as I told you. He has only been dead six weeks, so Rupert was busy tidying up his affairs of estate. As soon as all was settled, he travelled to London to keep an eye on me. My moving away was always a strain on the two of them and, although Rupert is younger than me, he is intent on looking out for me. With nothing holding him back, he decided to move closer to me. We are in the process of looking at suitable properties that we may move in together. He is also looking for a job in the city, though he has not yet managed to get an interview."

"Does he know anyone in London?"

"No, my father owned a small mill in Lancashire. Rupert worked on the firm's accounts and to my knowledge never travelled. He has never mentioned anyone in London and I am sure that if he had acquaintances here, I should know about them. Our relationship is very trusting."

"Do you know who has kidnapped him?" asked Holmes calmly.

The woman looked up in horror, "Obviously not, Mr Holmes. If I knew who the people were, I would not need your assistance now, would I? What is it you are trying to suggest?"

I could see the anguish on the face of the woman in that one moment, before it fell back to one of grief. "I assure you that I mean no harm in the question, Miss

Hekaltey. I can see it to be quite evident that you have nothing to do with this whatsoever. However, I do believe you know something that you are keeping to yourself. I assure you that I can be of no assistance unless the complete facts are given me. I have little time to waste."

I gave Holmes a sharp look but the woman was already beginning her answer. "There is one thing, Mr Holmes. I think it little to do with the case, but it gives me fright just to think about it."

"Please do continue, the merest detail is often the one that leads to a successful conclusion," prompted Holmes in his singularly calming tone.

"Well, my father wrote me a letter some weeks before he was taken ill. It is, or I should say was, unusual for him to write, for his hand was not perfect. So you can imagine that I was somewhat surprised to read his correspondence. He was worried about Rupert, and so he must have been if he had cause to put pen to paper. He said that Rupert had fallen in with some strange company which had turned his manners. My father was at his wits end about what to do, so pleaded for me to travel home to have a talk. This I duly did, when I had a weekend free from work. I sat with Rupert on a warm Saturday evening, on the edge of a field we had played in as children. We talked for hours, in that intimate way only a brother and sister can. Nothing could have been hidden from me and so it was with some horror that I listened to his tale. 'I have found a new spiritual path, Sister,' he said, 'I despair at father's scorn of anything but the material and I cannot help but feel that he has forced me into my current course of action. I can tell you no more.'

"You can imagine, Mr Holmes, my feelings at not being privy to his inner most secret – a secret that, I fancy, was most sinister. But as much as I pressed for an explanation, the harder his resolve became. In the end I could do little more than take his word that he would hide whatever his secret was from my father and not give him cause to worry. That was how it was left when I returned to London. Although little else was on my mind until I heard the news of father's illness, the grave news consumed me with grief and I had all but forgotten it until now."

Miss Hekaltey was controlling herself with admirable determination. I could feel the terrible chain of events as if I had endured them myself, it was all I could do, not to break down in sorrow at the sad tale. The remarkable story had a similar effect on Holmes, I fancy, for I could see in the briefest of moments a glaze fall over his eyes. The moment passed so quickly, I half thought I had imagined the expression, however, for no sooner had he turned and blinked then he said, "I do believe this could have a great bearing on the case. I am particularly interested in what your brother had to say about the spiritual and the material. There are two possibilities, but given the queer and most worrying turn of events, I can discount the theory that he had become involved in some intellectual grouping of philosophers arguing between the empiricist and the idealist schools of thought. Yes, I do believe we have a working hypothesis building before our very eyes and, if my suspicions prove to be correct, I should warn you that your brother is indeed in grave danger. We have no time to lose, but before we visit the Battersea boarding house I should like to ask one last question."

"Certainly, Mr Holmes," replied the woman in a strained tone.

"How did your father die?"

"It was an acute case of food poisoning. The doctors seem somewhat baffled as to the specifics."

CHAPTER TWO
The Black Cloak

The boarding house in Battersea was set slightly back from the road, protected at the front by a large hedgerow through which entrance was made by way of a wooden gate that creaked on its hinges. Whilst myself and Miss Hekaltey were shown into a small parlour by the landlady, Holmes began his search of the grounds. He was gone half an hour and on his return had that sharp gleam in his eye. "Miss Hekaltey, I assume your brother's room was on the first floor?" he said.

"Yes, that's right. It is just at the top of the stairs, the first on the right," she replied.

"Just as I thought," Holmes mumbled to himself, "I think it is time we had a look at this room."

With some encouragement, Holmes did manage to get the somewhat apprehensive Miss Hekaltey to accompany us to the room. It was small, with walls that had been painted ebony, which had a morbid effect. The feeling of confinement was enhanced by the amount of personal possessions that lay about the room in disorderly fashion. The bed had been slept in and had not been remade, the thin mattress having been indented heavily in the middle. There was one small window, that was firmly shut, overlooking the small garden and the alley that ran parallel to the house. On the opposite side of the alley were the grounds of a magnificent gothic church. The floor boards creaked as we all three walked across to the window, the floor was bare save the small rug that rested to one side of the bed. I sensed the fear in our client as Holmes began his methodical examination.

"I fear you are not comfortable in this room," I said to Miss Hekaltey.

"I am able to cope, Dr Watson. I have a certain dread of looking at my beloved brother's belongings, but am willing to do anything to take him away from harm," she replied quickly.

"Perhaps you would be so good as to arrange for us to take tea and ask the landlady if she would answer some questions," Holmes interrupted suddenly. "I think it best if I am left to work on my own, away from emotions," he continued when she had left the room.

By the time Miss Hekaltey and the tea had arrived, Holmes had made some preliminary conclusions, of that I was sure. He pulled a large, black piece of material from under the bed. It was impossible to make out what it was until he had unfolded it and held it aloft. Before I had chance to take in fully the discovery, our client had been overcome and slumped heavily to the floor. I managed to help her regain consciousness with difficulty, the colour from her face having drained completely. Her hands shook uncontrollably and she twitched as I tried to hold a cup of sweet tea to her lips. Once she had taken some of it, I helped her up and rested her on the edge of the bed with her back to the material that had brought on such a violent reaction. It was only when I was sure she had recovered sufficiently that I turned to Holmes who, far from seeming to notice the incident, was holding the material close to his eye and scrutinising it in great detail.

"What is it, Holmes?" I whispered.

He held it aloft once more and I recognised it as a large cloak. It had the appearance of a monk's habit, but the emblem emblazoned to its centre sent my blood cold. Although difficult to give an accurate description, for I know not what the pattern was supposed to represent, the violent lines and entangled thorns would strike fear into any person of sensibility.

"I think this is our first certain clue, especially given the effect it has had on our client. You would agree it is somewhat out of the ordinary?" said Holmes.

"It is horrible, Holmes, quite horrible," was all I could say.

"Ah, but that is not all, Watson. If you would be so good as to escort our client to the parlour where she may recover in the warmth, I should like to show you something else."

Miss Hekaltey didn't seem to hear Holmes and was genuinely shocked when I eased her up from the bed. Her eyes were glazed and she mumbled incoherently. She stumbled, even with my support, not saying anything. When I had positioned her in front of the parlour's fire, I returned to the bedroom to find Holmes rummaging through a chest I had not previously noticed in the corner. I looked over his shoulder at the mass of items in the chest. There were old books, a few articles of clothing, a photograph of Miss Hekaltey and some envelopes addressed to Rupert Hekaltey in a feminine hand. Holmes looked each one over briefly before discarding it onto the floor next to the chest. It was only when he held a large envelope in his hand that he stood up.

"Ah, Watson. I think we may have two more clues." He threw the envelope to the bed, upon which I could see that there was a seal in much the same pattern as that on the black cloak, but Holmes left the envelope and retrieved the cloak from the floor. "Here, look at this, and tell me what you make of it," he said as he rummaged into the bundle and pulled out a single triangular shape of black material. When he held it up, a feeling of horror ran through my nerves. It was one of the most singularly terrifying objects I had ever had the misfortune to set eyes on. I recognised it as a mask of some kind. It was of a dark colour and when opened up was much the same shape as a cone except for the frontal piece that was designed to drape over the face where two circles were cut out for the eyes.

"Holmes, I have never in all my life seen such a distressing object. What on earth is it used for?"

"Ah, now there are many distinct possibilities in answer to your question. We have to ask who it is that wears masks, and there are two answers. Firstly, and most obvious, is the person who does not want to be recognised – but why? The first possibility is that we have stumbled across criminal activity. However, there is one point that would lead me away from such a conclusion – the emblem stitched into the cloak seems unique, and one that would easily lead to positive identification. No, Watson, it is not merely that young Master Hekaltey was involved in criminal activity. Which brings us to the other, more sinister, possibility. If you would re-call the case some years ago of The Five Orange Pips, there are groupings who use masks, not only to hide their identity, but to put the fear of God into people. In that case it was the American secret society called the Ku Klux Klan – a most powerful and vicious group who used their power for political purposes, principally for terrorising negroes, murdering and driving from the country all those who were opposed to its views. If I recall correctly, they actually took their name from the sound produced by the cocking of a rifle. They use masks such as these to frighten and warn, as well as to disguise themselves in their murderous deeds."

"So we are dealing with a secret political grouping, resembling, if not actually being, the Ku Klux Klan, and this group is responsible for the kidnap of Rupert Hekaltey," I said.

"Well, Watson, that could be so, however I doubt very much whether it is the Ku Klux Klan themselves. They are most often to be found in white robes. I mean, it would not do for a group with such an aversion to our negro brothers to be seen in black robes, would it?" Holmes allowed himself a smile at his humour, a hu-mour that, I must say, I thought in slightly bad taste. "And as for their motives in forming a secret society, I think this envelope should give us a clue."

Holmes took the envelope from the bed and turned to me but, just as he opened it up, his eyes fell onto the cloak and he lost himself in thought. "What is it, Holmes? Why do you not open the envelope?" I asked.

He remained silent while he picked the cloak and mask up, holding each in a different hand and turning them over and over before his all-encompassing stare. "Watson – What do you make of the difference between the cloak and mask?"

"I fear I see little difference aside from one drapes over the body and the other over the face."

"Take a closer look. Observe, instead of wasting your time on the obvious," Holmes said sharply, pushing the two bundles into my arms.

"Why, there is a difference in them, Holmes," I suddenly exclaimed, having looked them over thoroughly. "Although they are of the same material, one is a slightly different shade. The cloak is lighter than the mask which is positively diabolical."

"Exactly, Watson. But be careful in conclusions drawn from the colouring. It is not that they were made in different colours, but that the cloak is older than the mask, it has faded in time, whereas the mask is almost brand new. This may mean nothing, however, for it could merely be that our client's brother has only recently acquired the mask to replace an old one, but, if this was the case, would we not expect to find the old one here too?"

"Yes, I suppose we would," I conceded.

"Indeed, so it might be that this secret society has not been in the habit of wear-ing masks until recently. It is an hypothesis and one that we can work on until we are able to disprove it. Now, let us take a look at the contents of this envelope." Holmes quickly opened it up and pulled out a single sheet of foolscap, careful to hold it from the sides in case there was a clue he might smother on the paper. "Well, it is a German paper, we can see that from the watermark and the colour and thickness, a combination not popular in England," he said, holding it to the light of the window. A look of confusion spread across Holmes's brow as he began to read. When he was finished he sat on the bed, lost in his own thought, and offered me the paper. The writing made little sense to me, made up, as a lot of it was, with seemingly meaningless characters. The whole message read:

The Order of the G.D.
(Dominus Liminis – the link)
Philosophus 4^0 = $7^\square$
Practicus $\quad 3^0$ = $8^\square$
Zelator $\qquad 2^0$ = $9^\square$
Neophyte $\quad 1^0$ = $10^\square$
Probationer 0^0 = $0^\square$

I turned to Holmes for some explanation, but his mind was elsewhere. He sat with his chin in his hand, struggling for an explanation. Eventually, I asked him, "What the devil does all this mean, Holmes?"

"Ah, quite a coincidental use of the word Devil, Watson, for I fear that what we have stumbled upon is an organisation that has had such accusations of witchcraft cast upon it, although the members themselves would strongly deny it."

"So you know who it is then, Holmes?" I asked.

"If I am not very much mistaken, the group calling themselves the Golden Dawn is implicated, though in what way I could not say at this stage."

"Who, or what, is the Golden Dawn?"

"They are romantics, Watson, mere romantics. But, among their secret membership, you would be surprised to find some of the most eminent men in London. Although not technically witches, they are practitioners of the ancient art of Magic, believing, as they do, that ceremony and ritual leads to higher planes of existence. It is something I have no time for but, nevertheless, strongly adhered to by some."

Holmes's face was solemn and his hands twitched as thoughts raced through his mind. He had turned a shade paler than his normal sallow complexion and his spine seemed to arch into a hunch before my very eyes. It was as if the life had been sucked from him. I was worried at this sudden withdrawal, not to say alarmed at the circumstances under which it had been brought about. My only course of action was to coax him back through questions relating to his other, if indeed there were any other, discoveries.

"So what does all this mean, Holmes? Is this all we have to go on, a witch's costume and a letter of mumbo-jumbo?"

"No it is not all, Watson, though I should take care to be wary of the power these people have," he replied, jumping up, suddenly full of life. "There are some other facts that I should draw your attention to before we return to Baker Street.

Let me begin by saying the story of kidnap is indeed correct and the place of kidnap was within this very room, carried out by two persons only. There has been a struggle by the bed, in one spot only. There are footmarks which correspond to this. Two men, one of large and heavy build and one smaller and lighter, somehow came into this room, whereupon they set about the kidnap while Mr Hekaltey slept soundly in his bed. After this struggle, I deduce that the victim was drugged in some way and they made good their escape through the window."

"I can see your method, Holmes, but surely you are wrong about the window; if I am not very much mistaken, it is nailed in place."

"How then, Watson, would you account for the footmarks in the earthen bed below and, more importantly, the flattened grass on the lawn that corresponds in all respects to a large object resting there?"

I fear you are mistaken, Holmes, look at this," I replied as I walked towards the window. I pointed to some scratched marks on the inner side of the wooden frame, "Not only is the window nailed in place but the perpetrators of this ghastly affair had a good attempt at opening the window before they gave up and made good their exit via another route. The marks you have observed outside must be coincidence."

"Ah, Watson, you believe exactly what they want you to believe. To illustrate my point, I should ask whether you have ever read the story of the Murders in the Rue Morgue?"

"Well of course I have, it is one of Poe's most ingenious stories. Indeed on many occasions, I have enlikened your good self to the character of Monsieur C Auguste Dupin in that same book."

"I should think I have better things to pursue than those of the out of control monkey, Watson, but you should recall the way in which the orang utang made its escape through seemingly nailed windows."

"Well, they appeared to be nailed but in the end were found not to be. Only the head of the nail was in the wood, not the full length."

"Exactly," said Holmes. He took a step towards the window, braced his hands on the lower part of the frame and, with that great hidden strength of his, pulled it open. The head of the nail stayed in place and on careful examination, it could be seen that the tip of the nail only scratched at the surface of the inner frame.

"Quite unimaginative, Watson. The perpetrators have not looked further than a library for a way of covering their tracks. So we know that they have drugged the victim after a struggle, disposed of the body by throwing it from this window before following it themselves, whereupon they made their retreat into the back alley, across the church yard and away on the road towards the river. There is surely some sinister group behind the plan, that may or may not have something to do with the secret sect of the Golden Dawn. There is another singular feature about the room that leads to an even greater suspicion of an occult group at work and that is the positioning of the window to overlook the churchyard. When we entered the room, I noticed first the shadow of the cross from the top of the spire falling onto the floor. I should think the room was picked by Mr Hekaltey for this reason. We have found much to work with, Watson, and after a brief talk with the landlady, we shall return to Baker Street and think through our next move."

I fetched the landlady from the parlour where she had revived Miss Hekaltey to as good a humour as possible given the circumstances. Holmes offered the landlady a seat on the bed before beginning his questions. She was a stout woman, well into her middle years, with a face that radiated a good humour. She smiled at Holmes as he raised his eyes to address her.

"Now, you are Mrs Hunter, proprietor of this house?"

"That is right Mr Holmes. And may I say what an honour it is to have such a remarkable and distinguished gentleman as yourself visit the house."

"You are too kind, Mrs Hunter, but I should like you to recall the events of last night, as you heard them."

"Well, I am an early riser, Mr Holmes, so I get myself to bed at an early hour. I did so last night, the same as usual and thought nothing of Mr Hekaltey. I could hear him in his room as I passed on upstairs, for my room is on the second floor directly above this one. I suppose I had long since been asleep when I heard some bumping from beneath. This was not unusual you understand, for Mr Hekaltey was most peculiar in his habits. I took little notice, even when I heard him open the window. I can say little more, for I am sure I drifted back to sleep."

"And at what time did you hear all this?" asked Holmes.

"It was in the early hours of the morning, I could not tell you exactly, but I should say around five o'clock. The sun was not up, but it was showing its first light as shadows came through my own window."   ·

"Thank you, Mrs Hunter. I think we have enough to be dwelling on. We shall return if we require anything further from you."

"You will always be welcome, Mr Holmes," replied the landlady as she followed us down the stairs.

Miss Hekaltey was waiting for us when we reached the front door and, amid our objections, insisted she was to make her own way home. She left the address of her lodgings in Brixton and bid us farewell. I was about to go through the doorway when Holmes turned once more to the landlady and asked, "Mrs Hunter, is that your own decoration in the bedroom?"

"What, the black? No, it most certainly is not. Young Mr Hekaltey begged me to let him paint it, when he first arrived. I refused at first but relented when he paid me some extra rent on the promise he would redecorate the room once he had departed."

"Thank you, Mrs Hunter, that is most interesting," replied Holmes.

CHAPTER THREE
Mycroft Holmes

Far from returning straight to Baker Street, Holmes and myself detoured via the Strand to lunch at Simpsons. The large oak panelling in the main restaurant, partitioned into cubicles, gave us an intimacy that had been rare on recent visits away from the Baker Street apartment. There was, however, a gloomy cloud hanging over the luncheon and, whereas I took more than my fair share of succulent sirloin beef, Holmes hardly touched his. He was withdrawn and spoke not a word between the time when our meal had been served and whence the table had been cleared. It was only when we were both on our second cup of tea and had our pipes firmly packed and lit, that Holmes seemed to shake off his grave reverie. He lifted his head quickly, letting his eyes open wide, and leant over to put a fond hand on my lower arm.

"You must excuse me, Watson. My behaviour over luncheon must seem intolerably rude," he said softly. For the briefest of moments, I fancied I could see a touch of sadness in his eyes.

"You must not think an apology necessary, Holmes. I should be glad to hear what is on your mind."

Holmes withdrew his hand quickly and dropped his head. For a moment I fancied I had forced him back into his own company but, just as I waved a hand for the bill, he began to speak. "This is a bad business, Watson, a very bad business," he said ruefully. "Although it appeared to be a unique case, and, of course, it is, I think I will have some very hard decisions to make in the next few hours. It is a very bad business indeed. I do believe I will come to regret taking the case from that poor girl."

"Holmes! You are surely not going to give up?" I said suddenly, "I have never known you give up on a case – besides, young Miss Hekaltey is depending on you to do your best. I have never known such a terrifying experience fall on a girl of such tender years."

"Yes, you are right, Watson, I must confess that my own feelings for Miss Hekaltey caused me to say this, I shall not give up the case under any circumstance. My professional – if not whole – life depends on my ability to solve criminal mystery and if I should fail without using every source available to me, so I should take it very hard indeed. Of that you can be sure. I do not care to protect any person from the force of the law, but I fear that a successful conclusion to this case may well put us in exceptional difficulties, and me especially. I do not fear to do my duty where there is evil to be conquered, Watson, and I hope to all heaven I shall be proved wrong in my preliminary conclusions. For if they prove to be correct, I shall undoubtedly lose someone close to me. Still, I must not dwell on such things. We must return to Baker Street, after sending a telegram, and then all shall be made clear to you."

Upon this strange concluding remark, I looked across at my friend and companion, Sherlock Holmes. He was putting on a brave face, but for what, I could not, for the life of me, guess. I realised the futility of asking any further questions, so followed him from the restaurant, down the Strand and into a hansom cab. Holmes ordered the cab to be pulled up at the lower end of Baker Street, whereupon he informed me he was sending a telegram and would make the rest of his way by foot.

By the time we were both in the front room of our apartment, a clock in the distance could be heard striking six in the evening. Holmes immediately lost himself in a stack of papers which I assumed to relate to the case we had spent the day turning over. I knew this to be correct when I caught a glimpse of one of the sheets full of symbols and expressions similar to those we had found on the sheet of paper in the trunk at Battersea. I lit a pipe and busied myself with some professional correspondence of my own, leaving Holmes to himself. We had a light dinner, for I, at least, was still feeling the effects of the fine food at Simpsons. I ate quietly, while Holmes made complaints about the thickness of the ham and the unevenness of the bread. He was in deep thought, which seemed vexatious in the extreme. When he did speak, it was sharply and when he moved back to the fire, he thumped his feet down hard on the floor. He spent the next hour pacing from one side of the room to the other. He frequently parted the curtain and peered into the street before turning quickly on his heels and pacing to the far wall, where he would flick a finger at flakes of plaster that had become slightly dislodged by his wayward revolver practice. Occasionally, he would pick up the violin and scrape a sequence of notes in a key reserved for those modern composers who can think up little that is a melody to the ears. Eventually, I could take no more, I offered to take myself off for a quick stroll.

"A stroll!" cried Holmes, "I thought you would be more interested in carrying through this case – since we are expecting a visitor any moment." I decided to stay and was glad to hear the sound of the front door opening, as it brought Holmes back to his chair where he lit a cigarette from the end of the one he had already half smoked. We had no time to wait for our visitor, for no longer than it took me to stuff and light my pipe had the door flung open and a large man stalked in. The only thing that was not huge about this man was his grey watery eyes, for the rest of him literally towered over anything else in the room, though his face had kept that sharpness of expression that could be seen all too readily in the face of his brother, Sherlock.

Mycroft Holmes had only visited us once before in a case where the Prime Minister himself was involved. Like his brother Sherlock, Mycroft had quite remarkable powers of observation and deduction. Indeed, it was Sherlock himself who conceded that his older brother had by far the greater powers of deduction, but was flawed in that he rarely moved from one of his three chairs. His three chairs being one in his own lodgings in Pall Mall, another in his place of work in a Government Office and, finally, one in his club, The Diogenes Club, which is quite the oddest club in London.

"Good evening, Dr Watson," said Mycroft as he extended a large hand in my direction, "I see you have been dealing with a case of rather rare infection and that the outcome was not favourable."

"By the laws of ... How did you know that?" I spluttered.

"Come now doctor, it is surely evident that you have been wearing protective gloves from the slight markings on your wrist, and I do believe the small trinket you hold in your hand to be a gesture of appreciation for attempting to prevent the departure of a loved one."

I looked down at the small gold figurine I had been, quite unconsciously, rolling around in my palm. "You are quite right, Mycroft. A sailor died at the docks last evening from some tropical disease that had carried off other crew members. But please tell me how you have been keeping."

"Very well, Dr Watson, I trust you have been keeping my young brother away from more trouble than he is capable of taking on?"

I did not have time to answer however as Sherlock sprung from his chair and spoke sharply, "I have not brought you here for polite conversation, Mycroft, so I should be rather grateful if you would have the courtesy of listening to what I have to ask you."

Both myself and Mycroft were somewhat taken aback by this sudden and quite unnecessary outburst. I glanced across to Sherlock who had his eyes fixed firmly on Mycroft; following the stare, I could see that the reverse was true. The two of them remained deadlocked in silence for some moments while an atmosphere of sullen awkwardness descended on the room.

"You have made good time from Pall Mall, Mycroft. I take it you left at twenty to eight as is your routine?" said Holmes eventually, but he kept his granite-like harsh expression.

"That is correct, Sherlock. I deduced the appointment must have been important for I know how you normally respect the habits of a lifetime for what they are. It must be something of utmost urgency for you to call me in, yet alone at such short notice. Pray proceed with anything of which I may be of assistance."

"I shall come straight to the point, Mycroft; I believe that our paths may cross in the course of my current case."

I looked both at Sherlock and Mycroft. Both had the sternest of expressions – as if they had remembered some old antagonism.

"Do continue," Mycroft replied without moving anything other than his thin lips.

"I believe you will be able to explain something of this to me?" continued Holmes as he retrieved the sheet of foolscap we had found in the trunk from his pocket.

All around us there was stillness. It seemed that even the people taking an evening journey down Baker Street had ceased to walk or drive in order that they could afford us an atmosphere of complete tension. The silence was broken occasionally by the crackle of flame in the fire place, but this occasional noise seemed to disappear from my conscious mind as I put all my effort into studying the expression on Mycroft's face. I could see his eyes following the six or so lines as they travelled down the page. Once at the bottom his eyes returned to the top and began again. This process was repeated three times until, on the fourth time, Mycroft's skin seemed to erupt violently with small beads of sweat, becoming larger as they joined with each other and rolled from his cheek, neck and arms. I held my breath for what seemed like an eternity, ready to come to Mycroft's assistance should he need any medical help.

I was glad when the silence was broken, but only for that split second in which I was ignorant of the ferocity of Mycroft's voice. "Where did you find this, Sherlock? It is none of your business. I demand to know how it happened to fall into your hands!" Mycroft's face was flushed with rage, while Sherlock Holmes maintained a steady gaze on his brother.

"So I take it that you do know what the paper is, then?" replied Holmes calmly. But Mycroft had risen to his feet and had raised his fist as if to strike the sitting man. Holmes did not flinch, but motioned his hand to Mycroft who promptly sat down again.

"You know very well that I should know the meaning of this paper, Sherlock," said Mycroft in cold tone, "And I doubt very much if you need me to tell you what it is. I would be much obliged however, if you could explain to me how it came to fall into your possession."

"That is of little importance until I know exactly what it is."

"Then I can be of little help, Sherlock, if you want to know, then use that re-markable deductive mind I read of so often."

At the same time, I wanted both to be away from the horrid tension in the room and to know the outcome and, indeed, the meaning of this queer conversation. I feared that the matter would remain unresolved as Mycroft let the paper fall to the floor and made as if to leave the room.

"It is some sort of ceremony conducted in the Sect of the Golden Dagger," said Holmes quickly.

Mycroft, who had risen to his feet and was walking to the door, stopped dead in his tracks and without turning said, in a voice that I can only describe as diabolical, "You know how to offend, Sherlock, I will give you that. I would advise you to rid yourself of that paper or give it back to the person from whom you have taken it upon yourself to steal."

Holmes did not reply until Mycroft had his hand on the handle of the door, but then said, "How could I give it back, when the person it belongs to has been kid-napped under the most violent circumstances."

This exclamation was enough to make Mycroft turn round. As he sat down once again, he said, "Kidnapped? I think you had best explain."

"The initials G.D. do not stand for the Golden Dagger, as I suggested, is that not so?"

"The initials are representative of the Golden Dawn, as well you know, Sherlock.

But to give the full title, it is Isis-Urania Temple of the Golden Dawn in the Outer. The sheet you have shown me gives the names of the ranks of initiates into the Order. It is only available to a select few. Indeed, I did not know of some of the titles of rank, there recorded."

"What – you mean to say, that you are involved in this secret society!" I suddenly exclaimed, unable to hold my tongue. Sherlock gave me a stern look, but Mycroft answered me genially enough.

"That is right, Dr Watson, but you would be well advised not to judge the society on what some of its critics have written in the press. I would also ask for your utmost discretion when you hear the information I will give you, I know I can trust it with you so it shall go no further. We, of the Golden Dawn, are all highly respectable people who share a common goal in wanting to know the way of nature. We do not believe that these great advances in technology amount to true knowledge – they take us away from the point of understanding the world around us. It is difficult to explain to a non-initiate and, besides, we do not have much experience at explaining. It is essential we can trust each other and keep our activities secret. There would be many people in England today who would think it to the benefit of all others if our activities ceased. It is simple really, we offer another, different, view. We are strong and stand up to those ideas that lead us into a shallow way of life. We are a grouping of the occult. We believe in, and practice, the ceremonies and rituals of magic that have been passed to us throughout the centuries. Now I have kept my end of the bargain, I would be obliged if you would give me the details of the kidnap."

I sat back and listened to Holmes recount the events of our extraordinary day. He left not one detail from the tale, mentioning in full the note from the kidnappers, the cloak, the mask and the hypothesis on the kidnapping. The face of Mycroft became more grave with every extra word spoken thus. When Holmes had finished, there was a short silence broken in the end by Mycroft letting out a huge sigh before beginning. "Your powers of deduction seem infallible, Sherlock, and I congratulate you on remembering the conversation we had over ten years ago when I first encountered the Golden Dawn. You are of course correct in your hypothesis, that the blame would fall at our group's door. If everything you say is correct, then this matter is very grave, very grave indeed."

"So you think it possible that the Golden Dawn is responsible?" asked Sherlock.

"I am in two minds as to how I should answer that, Sherlock. From my point of view, as a member with knowledge of the society, I would stand by my word that the Golden Dawn has had nothing to do with this event. We have some of the most respected men and women of England among our ranks. It would not do for them to be involved in something like this. However, I am at one with you, if I am objective and think about the evidence you have presented me. In that case, I would put my word on the Golden Dawn being responsible, though I cannot for the life of me think why. But I do have to concede that we have more than two hundred members and there is a possibility of a bad apple in there somewhere. As to this

Rupert Hekaltey, I have never heard the name before tonight. I should be much obliged if you would give me some idea of what your next move is to be."

"I will be willing to let you have that information in a minute, but before that I should like to show you this," said Sherlock, handing Mycroft the notices in the day's paper, "What do you make of it?"

Mycroft looked at it for some considerable time, his brow furrowing as he tried to reach his conclusion. He handed it to me without a word and I saw that Holmes had circled one of the notices. It said:

> ADEPTUS
> All is in place.
> Proceed as discussed.
> The German opponent has lost his pawn.
> DEMON EST DEUS INVERSUS

I had no idea what this could mean, though it had a somewhat curious effect on Mycroft. He hung his head, rolled his eyes and began to gasp for breath. Holmes was the quickest to react, rolling up a sheet of paper that fitted as snug as a mask over Mycroft's face. For some minutes Mycroft breathed in and out, until the rhythm became more regular and the attack of over-ventilation had passed.

"I must apologise," said Mycroft on regaining the ability to communicate, "There is, as you say, something happening within the Order. It is evident, as you have noticed, Sherlock, that someone within the Order is indeed responsible for this terrible deed. I am at your disposal for anything you wish to know."

"Firstly," said Holmes, "I should like to know the meaning of the message."

"Well," began Mycroft, "It would appear that this Rupert Hekaltey has been working with a man by the name of MacGregor Mathers. He was the founder of The Golden Dawn and has since moved to Germany. There is no secret in the Society that there is a rift between Mathers and the leaders here in England. Hence the message is from the kidnapper to other members of the Order, that they have taken one of Mathers' allies. I had not realised the gravity of this rift, it must be said, so I could not lead you any further than this, rather slight explanation."

"Is there no clue as to the person who signs himself as Demon Est Deus Inversus?"

"Not that I can help you with. It could be translated as, 'A Demon is an Inverted God'. I have not heard the expression before, of that you have my word, but my instinct tells me it is a black form of our art – not in practice amongst our main body."

"One other question, before I ask you to put your trust in my actions."

"Anything, Sherlock, I confess that I am ashamed of this sorry affair."

"What is the meaning of the masks?"

"This feud has led to a bitter battle for power. It has been suggested that complete anonymity should be maintained until such point as it is resolved. Consequently, some members, but by no means all, have taken the option of wearing a mask to all meetings. I myself do not believe in this action and am far from involved in the feud, so I refuse to wear one."

"But you have got one?" said Holmes eagerly.

"Yes I have one, but, as I say, I haven't used it."

"Ah, excellent," replied Holmes, "and when is the next ritual or ceremony?"

"Why, there is one I am due to attend this night, at the hour of twelve."

"In that case, you shall forfeit your mask and cloak to myself and I shall go in your place to see if I cannot make some progress in this case. As it is already ten o'clock, we shall have some tea and then you shall take me to the Order's meeting-place."

For a brief moment, I thought Mycroft was going to protest, but the eager anticipation and excitement in Holmes's eyes is surely one of the hardest things to disappoint. As it was, we finished our tea. I was finally left to my own company while Holmes and Mycroft departed at ten thirty.

CHAPTER FOUR
The Golden Dawn

The Baker Street flat felt empty and unused whenever Sherlock Holmes was out. It was especially so on this dark and windy night. He had left with his brother Mycroft at ten thirty and I had stayed up, occupying my mind with the trivial matters of tidying and ensuring my diaries were in order. This activity had taken little more than two hours and, once it was finished, I was again plunged into a state of nervous anticipation due to the long wait. But, this was no ordinary wait, for, unlike on most previous occasions, I knew exactly where Holmes had been heading. I felt fresh anxiety as the clock struck that single chime of one o'clock. The next sound was that of two o'clock and even the hour of three made itself heard before steps were audible on the stairs outside.

The door flung open and a caped figure came in. Only two grey eyes could be seen through the dark mask. Of course there was a certain amount of irrational fear in that first moment, for I knew that it must be Holmes. Had I not been privy to his intentions, however, I would never have guessed at the identity of the intruder. He was surely taller than Holmes, and proportionally, his figure was fuller, with the cape hanging off very broad shoulders. "Ah, Watson, I am surprised you waited up to this late hour," said the familiar voice.

At once, my mind was put at rest and I gave my reply as he struggled to pull the mask from his face, "You surely could not have expected me to sleep when I have had nothing to think about but your pursuit of those dreadful kidnappers."

"No, I suppose not," he conceded as he pushed the palm of his hands to the fire. The flames seemed to absorb all of his thoughts as he remained in this position for some minutes. He stood up straight when he had warmed himself enough and had come to the end of his thought process. "I shall go to change, Watson, and then we shall discuss the case. Maybe there is something I have overlooked." Holmes retired to his room. I settled myself in the chair to await his return, certain in my own mind that he had gained little from the night's visit.

Holmes returned, his face immobile, his jaw protruding and his lips pursed tightly together. His face was indeed grave and he stalked twice around the room before slumping into the chair opposite me and letting his tense expression fall from his face. I could see that his eyes were heavy and his cheeks were drawn in from exhaustion.

"I am afraid that I have not progressed as far as I would have liked tonight, Watson," he said once his pipe was lit.

"I would be much obliged if you might tell me how tonight progressed, Holmes," I said, unable to contain my curiousity any longer.

"Indeed Watson, it must have been quite a strain on your nerves having to wait for word when we have engaged with what we assume to be the enemy. I hope all this talk of witchcraft and the Devil has not disturbed you to too great a degree?"

"Nonsense, Holmes, that is what it is, complete nonsense. I fail to understand how such a respectable and otherwise sceptical man as Mycroft can become involved in this sort of thing."

"Ah, now there is the crux, Watson. I am inclined to agree with you when you refer to the whole business as nonsense, but nevertheless, no matter what we may think of the activities, a serious crime has been committed. As to my own brother, I think we must realise that our lives are fulfilled, mine with the pursuit of crime and yours with that worthy profession of medicine. Less fulfilled men may well be tempted into concerning themselves with what we would describe as nonsense."

"So where do we stand in the case, Holmes? Are you any closer to realising the identity of the kidnappers?"

"I am not sure, Watson. Tonight has proved to be disappointing but nevertheless most informative. I am not able to give you the precise whereabouts of the meeting place of the Golden Dawn, but it is in a large, most splendid house somewhere in the centre of London. When I arrived, some thirty other initiates were already present in a large room set at the back. No-one spoke to another but, rather, had their heads bowed in prayer. I was one of only four who wore the mask, all others were adorned in nothing other than their black cloaks. It was after some minutes that we were addressed by a tall man who had stood and walked into the centre of the room. 'It is time,' he said, after which each man and woman, of whom there were some ten, filed silently behind him. He led us to a small door, hidden amongst bookshelves on one side of the room. On opening this, there was a strong wind upon us, carrying with it a pungent odour of incense. It was utterly pitch black and it was not until I had passed through that I found myself on stairs leading down. Slowly, with each step on the damp, stone stairs, light began to seep up from the area below us. There were over one hundred steps down, so I calculated the depth of the cellar as around seventy five feet.

"The cellar was cold and was dimly lit with candles cut into the wall. It was a large space, possibly as much as one hundred feet across. At one end stood an altar, draped in white silk, with an exact opposite exposed at the other end. The initiates took their place around the edge of the room whereupon, once everyone was settled, three men picked candles from the wall and walked to the centre. They knelt into each other and began to speak in a tongue I am not familiar with, but what I deduced to have some origin in the north African countries. When they had finished, a general chant sprung up in the same tongue. Once I had memorised the sounds, I duly began to chant so as not to give myself away. The noise was deafening – it seemed to rebound off every wall right back into our faces, which showed me that the walls were solid and would not let any sound escape the room. While the chant was continuing, the three men had departed and were replaced by a masked man.

"This man held his arms up and immediately ceased the chanting from all the other initiates. He lifted his head up above his stooped body and began to speak. 'Fellow initiates,' he said, 'there is evil in the air, as we already know, and it is time to fight for our church. We have done nothing wrong, but we have to fight for what we know to be right. The wheels have already been put into motion and we will surely be victorious under the name of the Secret Chiefs.' As soon as he had finished speaking, the chanting began again. It continued for some half an hour while various rituals were carried out which involved little more than the passing of candles between people and a different chant springing up therein. It was then that I had a piece of good fortune for, when the meeting finished and we were on our way up the stairs, I noticed a key fall from the pocket of the man who had given the short speech. I picked it up without anybody noticing and pushed it into the lining of this cloak. That is all there is to say at this moment, Watson, if you have any questions, please feel free to ask in the morning, for I am now in need of a couple of hours sleep before I set about putting the wheels of our own investigation further into motion. Good night."

"Good night, Holmes."

It must have been soon after that moment that I fell asleep in the chair only to be woken by Holmes shaking me by the shoulder. "Watson, I need to talk to you before our client arrives," he said.

It took me a few moments to get my bearings before I realised that I had, indeed, not made it to my own room and had fallen asleep in a most uncomfortable position in the chair. The lower part of my back ached and my throat was dry from the raw smoke of the fire burning itself out in the early hours. "Our client, Holmes?" I croaked, "What time is it?"

"It is nine o'clock and I have just received a telegram from Miss Hekaltey, informing us she shall be arriving at ten. That leaves enough time for you to wash and have some breakfast."

On his word, I duly changed my clothes and sat down to breakfast. Holmes sat, lost in his own thought, turning a large key over and over in his hands. I joined him in a pipe just as Mrs Hudson announced the arrival of Tanith Hekaltey.

"Good morning, Mr Holmes and Dr Watson," the young lady said as she came in through the door. Holmes stood up and, taking her hand, led her to a chair before taking her overcoat and fur and placing it on the hat stand. I do hope you do not mind my disturbing you but I cannot concentrate on anything other than the progress I am hoping you will have made in trying to find my brother."

"Not at all, Miss Hekaltey, I will gladly give you all the information we have managed to gather on the case thus far. I was going to explain some of the happenings of last night to Dr Watson here, so you may as well hear what I have to say," replied Holmes in the kind manner he assumes on all too rare occasions. Holmes duly recounted the tale of the Golden Dawn and of his visit to their meeting, with a certain amount of pride. The colour seemed to return to Miss Hekaltey's cheeks with every word she heard, as if each was a comfort and that it would all lead to the inevitable return of her brother.

"Oh that is wonderful, Mr Holmes. I am so grateful for what you have done thus far, you are a most remarkable man," she said when he had finished.

It is all a case of logical deduction, Miss, there is no mystery in it," he replied, "though our work is far from complete."

"I have the utmost confidence in your ability, Mr Holmes, and I should be grateful if you would be so kind as to tell me of your next move. It is a great privilege to be so close to a man with such a brilliant mind as yourself."

I noticed these flattering words were not without effect on my friend. "Well, let me see now. As you will no doubt have gathered, my visit to the Golden Dawn was far from an overwhelming success, although it did go some way to proving my fears that they know more about this sorry affair than we can prove at this point in time. The leader, for I am sure that is what the masked man is, did everything but admit that they had been involved in the kidnapping. He talked of the battle and of wheels having already been put into motion. I am sure he is here referring to the kidnapping. I am in possession of the key to the house so I will endeavour to search the premises for I am sure they will yield, if not your brother, then a clue. But the first part of my day will be spent placing a notice in the Telegraph. This will confuse the kidnappers and force their hand, all that is then left is to wait for them to make their move and we shall be upon them."

"Wonderful, Mr Holmes, truly wonderful," cried Miss Hekaltey.

I turned to Holmes and saw a slight rush of blood briefly in his cheeks at the overwhelming praise he had elicited from our most beautiful client. I stood to fetch her coat as she also stood, but Holmes strode forcefully past me and grabbed her fur which he draped around her neck.

"Would you mind if I came tomorrow to check on your progress, Mr Holmes?"

"That would be most agreeable," Holmes replied.

Holmes departed half an hour later. I spent the afternoon visiting patients who had left messages during the morning. When I returned to Baker Street around the hour of six, I found Holmes in his chair, leaning back with his pipe and the day's paper.

"Ah! Watson, I would be obliged if you could have a look at this and give me your thoughts," he said before I had chance to remove my outer garments. I took the paper he offered me and began to read where he had been pointing. It was the notices column and I saw straight away another message:

ADEPTUS
Tread carefully.
The forces are mounting against us.
The pawn is soon to be worthless.
DEMON EST DEUS INVERSUS

"Holmes, this is terrible," I cried after I had read it through a number of times.

I fear they know we are on to them, Watson. I just hope they do not panic until the net is firmly set in place. There is nothing we can do except wait. I have spent the day productively. I am sure a successful outcome will be ours by this time tomorrow."

"Please explain, Holmes," I pleaded.

"With the help of the Irregulars and for the cost of not more than three pounds, I have discovered the place where the kidnapped person was first held. It is a small room attached to the cellar of the house I visited last night. I returned today and let myself in using this key." Holmes held out the key I had seen him handling the previous night, the key he had picked from the floor of the house. "The cellar, although seemingly solid, had two anti-chambers hidden in the stone walls, the doors of which are operated by levers encased in the wall. It was merely a matter of finding the correct stone that triggered the doors open, for the wall itself gave away the hiding place as it was made of a slightly more sandy type of stone. The stone, although looking the same in every respect, is a better conductor of heat and consequently felt warmer than the rest of the wall. One of these chambers had not been used recently, the hinges were rusted together so the door would not open more than a couple of inches, but the other one was well oiled and swung open easily once the switch was flung. Inside, the dust had not settled from the imprisonment. There were footprints on the floor, three sets, two of which were consistent with those found in the house at Battersea. From the lack of moisture on the floor, I should guess that the prisoner was removed not more than twenty-four hours previously. Indeed, he may well have been there during the ceremony I took part in last night, though I should think they did not dare take the risk when they knew we had started an investigation.

"I have taken out a notice in the *Telegraph* that will flush them from their hiding place. All we need to do is wait for their next move."

CHAPTER FIVE
The Double Notice

When I arose the next morning, Holmes was already up and about. He was pacing the room, his chin tucked tightly into his chest and his hands clenched at his side. On the table, by the side of the pile of untidy papers rested his revolver, cleaned and ready. The fire had already burned through its first helping of coal so I deduced that Holmes had been up for at least two hours, that is if he had retired to his room at all during the night. He did not seem to notice my entrance and continued to pace up and down. I ordered some tea and sat down with my pipe.

"Holmes, I wish you had some other way of expressing your nerves," I said when I could stand no more of his perpetual pacing.

"I apologise, Watson," he replied, taking his seat next to mine, "I am awaiting the delivery of this morning's paper and will not rest easy until I see that my trap has been laid."

Holmes removed his watch and checked the time. The single sovereign that he had been given by Irene Adler sparkled from its chain. "What is the time, then, Holmes?" I asked.

"It is half past eight and the paper should have been delivered by now. That is the front door is it not? I do believe it is here."

We both fell silent and listened for the footsteps of Mrs Hudson but, even with my own limited capability of deduction, I knew the footsteps that followed not to be of our landlady. They were hasty and heavy and, no sooner had I counted them to seventeen did the door fly open and a large man stormed into the room. On hearing the steps, Holmes had sprung to the table and picked up his revolver which I could now see pointing from his smoking jacket pocket at our new arrival. The man was followed by Mrs Hudson who skirted around his large frame and into the centre of the room.

"I'm sorry, Mr Holmes, I tried to stop him but he pushed me aside," cried Mrs Hudson with a certain degree of despair.

"That is quite all right, Mrs Hudson," replied Holmes coolly, "Perhaps you could make some tea for our unexpected guest. And perhaps you would be so good as to bring the morning's paper – as soon as it arrives."

"Very good, Mr Holmes."

"I have little time, Mr Holmes, for I am a very busy man," said the man suddenly. His voice was harsh but his accent was that of a professional man. He was well dressed and his shoes were new, unscuffed. In his hand he clutched a large leather bag and he quickly removed his hat to reveal a full head of silver hair. All in all, he had the air of a most distinguished gentleman.

"You had best explain your rude interruption then, Sir," replied Holmes quickly, "And then you will be able to take your rather old dog cart to the Temple."

The hard expression fell for a brief moment from the man's face as the accuracy of Holmes's deduction sunk in. He removed his coat and sat down in the chair normally reserved only for Sherlock Holmes.

"I say!" I said before I could help myself, "If you are going to push your way into our apartment and take the chair reserved for one of the country's greatest minds, I should like to know who you are."

"I am Mr Gill QC and I am not in the practice of making pleasantries with those who have stepped over the boundary of politeness in their own actions. As I said, I have little time and I would be grateful if Mr Holmes would explain his deplorable actions. If you have no satisfactory explanation for your conduct then I should be only too pleased to begin criminal proceedings against you."

I could feel that my mouth was hung open in a rather ungainly fashion, but could not bring myself to close it. I was shocked at what I had heard, and was not to be able to control my nerves. I am sure that if I was the one with the revolver in my pocket, instead of Holmes, I would have been unable to do anything but release a barrel into this arrogant man's chest. But Holmes was apparently unmoved by the extraordinary turn of events, he merely strolled to the vacant chair and proceeded to light his pipe from a small wooden splint he removed from the fire.

"You have lost me completely, Mr Gill. Surely there is some mistake, I have been called a lot of things in my time but never a criminal, and especially from someone who, like yourself, is firmly set on the right side of the law."

"That is not the case, Mr Holmes, as well you know. I have had the pleasure of following your career from a legal point of view and find myself hard pushed to justify some of the methods you have employed in the past. However, in the light of the results you have obtained, I have seen to it that I should overlook some of your less worthy actions, but this new incident cannot be ignored by myself and, if necessary, the police," replied Mr Gill angrily.

"Then perhaps you would be so good as to explain who your client is, and how I have offended them in such a way. I really cannot recall being on the wrong side of the law, but you are, after all, the expert so I should be happy to accept any explanation of which I was unaware."

"I think, Mr Holmes, that you are only too aware. Only too aware of the crime of house-breaking, is that so?"

I could see no change in the expression of Holmes except for a slight darkening of the eye and, I fancy, a brief turning up of the sides of his mouth as if he were about to smile.

"House-breaking? But of course I am aware of the crime of house-breaking and assure you once again that to my mind I have not stepped outside of the law."

"This is intolerable, Mr Holmes!" shouted the man suddenly, "You are wasting both my time and yours, I have never known such behaviour. You may, at least, have the decency to explain your despicable behaviour. You are guilty of breaking into a house yesterday afternoon!"

Holmes suddenly gave a start, pushing himself back into the chair, before regaining his composure and asking, "May I ask, once again, who your client is, Mr

Gill?"

"You know the identity, if not the name, of my client, Mr Holmes, so I suggest you come forth with your explanation quickly."

"So, Mr Gill, your client is the Golden Dawn?"

"They are my clients, Mr Holmes, yes and I am getting restless. I want to know why you took it upon yourself to break into the premises of my client, having deceived them the night befcre. I would also like to know what part your accomplice plays in this outrageous incident. I believe Mycroft Holmes is your brother?"

"Yes he is, though he has nothing to do with the charges you are levelling against me. If there is any responsibility – it is all mine – there have been some necessary actions in the pursuit of those men who have engaged in a most ghastly crime."

"Please do not say any more, Mr Holmes, else I should feel pressed to bring a case of slander against you. The Golden Dawn is a most respectable society and has, amongst its membership, some of the most respected men in the country. Your persistent harassment of them is absolutely unwarranted."

"Ah, so you would stand in the way of justice, you would protect those who have caused nothing but terror and fear for respectable members of the public?"

"Terror and fear!" thundered the man, I shall show you terror and fear by the time I have finished with you, mark my word and as to justice, your definition is highly unusual."

"I care not for your brand of sarcasm, Mr Gill, and I should like to know just how your definition defends the crime of kidnap," replied Holmes harshly. I could see that his temper was on the edge of being lost altogether.

"Kidnap? I know nothing of what you say, Mr Holmes," replied Mr Gill, suddenly unsure of his words. His chest had deflated and a look of bewilderment had descended over his features.

"That is correct, Mr Gill, there is a strong case to be made against the Golden Dawn. We believe them to have been involved in the kidnap and subsequent threat to one Rupert Hekaltey."

"I demand to know your evidence," cried Mr Gill.

"Ah, now why on earth should I divulge evidence to someone who may well be profiting from the crime in question? I strongly believe that the matter will be resolved before this day is out. I am not presently in a position to divulge any of my information."

Mr Gill's face had turned a deep shade of red and he was about to explode into reply when there was a knock at the door. Mrs Hudson entered with the tray of tea and the morning paper.

"Thank you, Mrs Hudson, I am sure that Dr Watson would be good enough to oblige with serving tea," said Holmes dismissively.

As I took the cups from the tray on the table, Holmes busied himself flicking through the pages of the paper. Our uninvited guest sat somewhat bewildered, unable to speak. I duly served him his tea whereupon Holmes gave a cry of surprise. He had the paper laid out in front of him and was looking aghast at the column of notices.

"This is serious, Watson," said Holmes after we had stared at him for some time
I looked across at Mr Gill. It was as if Holmes had completely forgotten his
presence and had reverted to addressing myself only.

"What is it, Holmes? I asked.

Holmes looked up from the paper and let it slide to the floor in front of him. His
face was the picture of torment. He gave a none too trusting look to our visitor,
who was himself looking thoroughly confused by the whole episode.

"It is the most horrendous thing I have ever read, Watson, that is what it is," said
Holmes in a cold voice, "But before I show you what has chilled me to the bone, I
should be most impolite if I did not give Mr Gill here an account of the sequence of
events that led me to having no option but to break into his client's property."

I listened to Holmes recount the tale of our case, once more. Mr Gill sat atten-
tively for the most part but occasionally protested at the impossibility of the accusations, claiming his clients' utmost respectability. Holmes, although recounting
some of his most remarkable deductive work, was strangely detached from the
words that he spoke. It was evident he was still thinking about the notice in the
paper.

"Mr Holmes, this is a preposterous tale you have told me, although I do now see
that there is a certain amount of justification for your actions. However, I can say
without any cause for concern, that my clients are completely innocent of the charge
you have brought against them and that you must have made some miscalculation
somewhere in your investigation."

Although Mr Gill's voice was still officious, it had softened considerably. He
took the cup of tea I had poured for him with a genial smile. "Thank you, Dr
Watson. I am sorry to trouble you with my abrupt entrance this morning, I was a
touch hasty in my conclusions, but you must understand how the situation looked
from my position." I nodded an acceptance of his apology and he turned to Holmes,
"Mr Holmes, I do hope you are not still of the idea that any of my clients, individu-
ally or as a whole, could possibly have any connection to this kidnapping."

"You have no need to fear, Mr Gill. Our investigation is complete," replied
Holmes absently.

"What," I cried, "The suspect has been captured?"

"There is no suspect, Watson, and there never was a kidnap," replied Holmes
gravely.

"You have lost me, Holmes," I said with some bewilderment.

"And me," said Mr Gill.

"Perhaps you may have a look at this then, Watson," said Holmes as he handed
me the paper from the floor.

I took the paper and looked at the column of notices. My eyes fell immediately
on a notice that had been taken on by my colleague. It said:

ADEPTUS.
There is nothing to fear.
A solution to our problem lies at 221B Baker Street.
Proceed there in all haste.
All will be evident.
DEMON EST DEUS INVERSUS

"I presume, Holmes, that you have placed this notice here," I said, accustomed to the many different methods my colleague employed to his own end.

"Yes, that is indeed the case, Watson. But the problem occurs later in the column. If you would care to let your eyes wander further, then no doubt all will become evident."

I did as Holmes suggested and was surprised to see another notice, in much the same style, it read:

ADEPTUS
Ignore previous notice.
Baker Street trickery.
DEMON

"But why should you wish to cancel your own notice, Holmes?"

"Ah, but it is not my notice, my dear Watson, rather the notice of some person who knew that my notice was going to be included in today's paper."

"I do not understand, Holmes, who the devil knew what your course of action was to be? And how do you know that there never was a kidnap? How do you explain the disappearance of Rupert Hekaltey?"

"Watson, I must make my explanation brief, for there may be a chance to apprehend the hoaxer, but needless to say, there never has been a man by the name of Rupert Hekaltey. Think – who knew that I was going to be taking out this notice."

"Only myself and you, Holmes, and I most certainly have nothing to do with this."

"Watson, you do not think. Think man, think man! Who else was present when I stated my intention?"

"Why only our client, Miss Hekaltey."

"Exactly! The woman who brought the case to our attention. After what Mycroft has explained to us about the feud in the Golden Dawn, it should be obvious, should it not, that our so-called client, Miss Tanith Hekaltey, is involved with those on the side fighting against the Order. By bringing our attention to a pretended, vile crime – never actually committed – she has enlisted us in an attempt to discredit the Golden Dawn. She heard of my intention, took it upon herself to visit the *Telegraph's* offices herself, and, by some deception, managed to discover the content of my message. Once knowing this, she had to warn off her accomplice, in case he should fall into the trap I had laid for him. Watson, we have been outwitted by a plausible woman and must waste no time in trying to track her down."

"I am glad to see that you no longer suspect my clients as having any involvement in this case, Mr Holmes," said Mr Gill suddenly.

Holmes turned towards him as if seeing him for the first time. "Ah, Mr Gill. I should apologise for my indiscretions and my rather harsh talk of earlier, but given the circumstances, I am sure you will agree when I say I had some justification."

"And so you did, Mr Holmes. I should surely be very grateful if you could help clear up this sordid mess. I am sure it is in both our interests for you to do so."

"I shall indeed commence my investigations, Mr Gill. You must excuse my abruptness, but if we are quick, we may be in time to apprehend this Scarlet Woman and her accomplice. I bid you good-day, Sir."

CHAPTER SIX
The Beast's Scarlet Woman

Holmes spoke little on our way to the boarding house in Brixton. He urged the driver to make haste which he duly proceeded to do, taking the corners with such speed as nearly toppled the cab more than once. We pulled up outside the address that had been given to Holmes by Tanith Hekaltey. It was a large house, with three stories in all, but lights came up from a small grate by the side of the front door, indicating that the basement was in use. A strong smell of onions also wafted up from below. Holmes tapped impatiently on the knocker.

"I'm coming, I'm coming. Hold your horses," came a voice from the inside. Seconds later the door was opened by a portly woman dressed in a blue apron. No sooner had she looked over us with an inquisitive eye then Holmes pushed past her. "Oi! You can't come barging in here like that sir," she shouted, "State your business. What the devil ......"

"Tanith Hekaltey, where is she?" replied Holmes sternly.

"She has left. Though, what may I ask is your business with her?"

"When did she leave?"

"Last afternoon," replied the woman, "And I have not had a reply to my question. What the devil is your business coming around here and pushing your way into private property?"

"I will explain if you could give us some of your time, Ma'am," said Holmes as he retreated back towards the door.

"Here how am I s'pposed to give you my time when I do not know who I am addressing?"

"My name is Sherlock Holmes and this is Dr Watson. It is most urgent we know something of your guest."

"Why, Mr Holmes, you should have said. Such a gentleman as yourself is only too welcome in this house. Would you like some tea?"

We both followed her into the parlour which was the nearest room, facing, as it did, the road. Even though the spring sun had been warming the air all morning, there was still a small fire crackling in the corner, about which there was a settee and two large, but slightly soiled, armchairs. Above the fire hung a large bore rifle. We were left to discuss the rifle as the landlady set about making us some tea. She returned with what I assumed to be her most precious silver salver. I settled back, with the fresh tea going some way to calming my nerves from the journey in the cab.

"Now ma'am, I wish to know all you have to tell me on your previous guest, Tanith Hekaltey, starting with when she arrived," began Holmes.

"I'm not sure I have that much to tell, Mr Holmes. She arrived two weeks ago to the day and left, as I have said, yesterday afternoon. She had paid for two weeks, but did not come to claim a refund for the extra day. I did not know she had left until I went to make up her room this morning, to find it deserted, all her belongings had been taken. As to anything else, I am sure I can be of little help. She was a very quiet girl, said she worked as a clerk in Ludgate and needed somewhere to stay while her husband went about finding suitable accommodation in Surbiton. Aside from that, there was nothing, I hardly saw her."

"You mentioned her husband, did he ever visit?" asked Holmes hastily.

"Just the once. He was a good looking young man, strong shoulders and deep dark eyes; though he only allowed me a quick glance before he covered his face with a large overcoat. That was all I could describe him as but later on I was sure I could hear them arguing. He left shortly after that."

"And when was this?"

"Last Wednesday, I am sure," replied the woman.

"Where was he staying?"

"That, I cannot tell you. Neither he nor Tanith spoke of a place to me, but I must say I found it a most queer situation that a man should not stay with his wife for such a short period."

"Indeed, most odd," agreed Holmes, "May I see her room?"

"Certainly, it is the second on the left on the first floor. It is vacant, I have a guest arriving to fill it tomorrow."

Holmes left the landlady and myself to talk of little but how brave her husband had been in Afghanistan and how all she had left of him was his hunting gun. I was on my second cup of tea when Sherlock Holmes returned.

"Our investigation here is complete, Watson, we must hurry to our next stop," he said.

"Before you go, would you tell me why you want to find Tanith," said the woman as we headed for the front door, but Holmes strode through the door and up the garden path in such a way as to make it obvious he was not in the business of giving an explanation.

"Where are we off to now, Holmes?" I asked once the driver had cracked his whip.

"We shall pay another visit to the boarding house in Battersea and I shall wire Scotland Yard to meet us there," he replied, before shouting, "Stop here, driver!"

Holmes bounded from the cab and disappeared into a post office to send a telegram. He was not gone more than two minutes and then we were off again. The driver held little back in the name of safety as the cab shot along the streets. We arrived in one piece, however, and Holmes strode purposefully to the front door. As I followed in his steps, another cart pulled up and a red-faced Inspector Lestrade ran past me. Holmes had knocked on the door, the only response from which was a brief twitch of the curtains on the first floor.

"Lestrade, we shall need to break the lock!" cried Holmes.

The Inspector took little time in summoning two policemen and giving them the task of ramming the door from its hinges. The first attempt failed, as the door did little but creak. Before the second attempt could be made, however, the door opened of its own accord and a bemused looking Mrs Hunter stood in the front hall.

"Has Miss Hekaltey been here?" demanded Holmes in rough tone.

"Not since you yourself were here," she replied. I could see her shaking from the ordeal and her face was contorting horribly under the pressure of her unexpected visit. I fancy that it was not the reappearance of myself and Holmes that worried the old woman, however, but the presence of the five or so uniformed policemen.

"I demand this woman be arrested, Lestrade," shouted Holmes angrily.

"On what charge, Holmes? She hardly looks the criminal type."

"No, Lestrade? Perverting the course of justice should be charge enough," spluttered Holmes in reply.

"Just hold on a minute, I have no knowledge of what you are saying, Mr Holmes. Perhaps it would be for the best if we went inside to discuss the matter calmly," replied Lestrade.

"I agree, Holmes," I suddenly intervened, worried at Holmes's temper. He muttered something to himself before consenting to holding a brief interview in the front room of the boarding house.

"Now, Sherlock Holmes, may we hear the details of the case you have been working on that brings you to this residence?" said Lestrade when all the officers had been furnished with cups of hot tea by the nervous Mrs Hunter. Holmes took little time in patching the case together as it stood and, at its conclusion, accusing Mrs Hunter of involvement with the conspiracy. "Well, what have you got to say for yourself, Mrs Hunter? The case seems to implicate you as an accomplice in trying to discredit an honourable, if unusual, society while it is involved in criminal court proceedings."

Mrs Hunter's cup shook to the point where one of the officers removed it gently from her hands and set it safely on a small wooden sideboard. It is not what you think, Sir. I had no idea of their true purposes. I am a poor woman who has little in life but my small income from occasional guests in this house. Tanith Hekaltey and a man, whose name I never knew, offered me good money to rent them the room. Well, you can imagine that I should have been a fool not to take the offer, but they insisted I should keep to the story they told me if anyone should ask. They painted the room black and, for all I know, placed all the objects you found. I duly kept my end of the bargain when I repeated what they told me to say to you, Mr Holmes. I swear that I knew nothing of some society. They told me they were friends of yours, Mr Holmes, and were repaying a practical joke you had played on them some time previously. The woman broke down in tears and the police officers looked to the floor in embarrassment. It was only Holmes who kept his eyes on the old woman. He stared at her in cold hatred, a look that made me shiver.

"Well, Mrs Hunter," said Lestrade eventually, "you should think yourself lucky this time, in as much as I shall not be taking this case any further. We have more important things to concentrate on than a case of common deception, but I should advise you to think of the consequences before you plunge yourself into another escapade of this kind."

We left Mrs Hunter to her dirty cups and shame. In the road, Lestrade approached the silent figure of Sherlock Holmes. "I have never been so embarrassed, Holmes. What on earth were you thinking of laying the blame on a poor defenceless woman like that? You should be ashamed of yourself. It is obvious that she was a victim of this practical joke as much as yourself. Is this the way the country's greatest detective behaves when he has been most convincingly outwitted?"

Lestrade departed with his men and we drove at a more sedate pace to Baker Street. Once safely back in our apartment, Holmes, who had not said a single word on the way home, busied himself preparing chemicals in the apparatus he had set up permanently in the corner of the room. I left him to it for a good few hours until it was he that broke the gloomy silence. He picked his pipe from the mantelpiece, poked in bad temper at the fire, and sat next to me.

"I have been such a fool, Watson, such a fool," he said. I looked up from the paper and noticed that his eyes had contracted and his cheeks were drawn. His long thin nose cast a depressing shadow over his chin as he hung his head. In short, he looked like an old man, the day had taken its toll on him and, with the knowledge he had failed in his latest case, he was already in a state of acute depression.

"It is surely not as serious as all that Holmes, after all, no harm has come," I replied.

"That is far from the point. I have been tricked into working for people who are operating on the wrong side of the law. It was all there to see, my vision has been blinkered and they ran rings around me."

"I hardly think that to be the case, Holmes. You are surely being too hard on yourself. Was it not your deduction that allowed us to realise the deception in the first place? I am sure that I would never have been able to think the truth had I been confronted by those two notices. What is more, I was also taken in by the young Tanith Hekaltey, she was most convincing in her part, we have to give her that."

"Stop, Watson!" cried Holmes, "That was my first mistake. Her name. It can surely not be Hekaltey." He jumped up, retrieved his trusted encyclopaedia from the book case and began to flip through the pages. "Heilbronn, Heirndall, Heine, Hejaz.... Yes, here we are, Hekate. The name of the ancient goddess of the underworld. The Germanic form of which is Hexe, being another name for a spell of magic. How blind I have been, Watson, I should have seen it from the start. In presuming a false name, our Scarlet Woman has constructed herself into a powerful figure in occult theory."

"Never, Holmes, who would have thought such a demonic thing?"

"Ah, now that is the mind of a most evil or, at least, misguided person, Watson, and I fancy, a clue as to the identity of her accomplice. He is a well built man, that much we know from the description afforded to us by the landlady of the Brixton boarding house and from the footprints found in the earthen bed of the Battersea house."

"But you said the supposed kidnap was carried out by two males. There were two sets of footprints."

"Indeed that is true, Watson, though I think that even in that instance I was tricked into believing there to be two men involved. With the evidence now apparent, the single line of information passing between only two people in the notices of the paper and both testimonies available to us, those of the landladies at Battersea and Brixton, I deduce that the second set of footprints were the marks of the Scarlet Woman, albeit she was not wearing her normal shoes. I must salute the capabilities of these two fraudsters. If it were not for my chancing on their only means of communication, I do believe we would have found ourselves in very hot water, Watson."

I accepted Holmes's explanation in wonder and it was not until he had returned to his chemical analysis with renewed vigour that I realised his depression had lifted slightly with his admiration of the tactics employed by the Scarlet Woman. Later, when I had taken some dinner and Holmes had decanted what must have been his hundredth flask, Mr Gill was brought in to us. Holmes immediately dropped what he was doing and waited in eager anticipation for our guest to take his place in the vacant chair.

"Mr Gill, it is good of you to give us some more of your valuable time," said Holmes amiably, once he had offered the barrister a cigarette. I trust you have brought the notes of your case with the Golden Dawn."

"I have done better than that, Mr Holmes. I have original copies of the complaint brought against the Golden Dawn. The complaint has been withdrawn and Scotland Yard have been good enough to allow me access to their documents."

"I would be much obliged if you could furnish me with as much detail on the case as your confidentiality allows, Mr Gill," replied Holmes quickly. His excitement was evident and he could barely contain himself from hurrying our guest along.

"Of course, Mr Holmes, you will understand that some of the points are still confidential, but I am able to give you a general outline. The society known as the Order of the Golden Dawn is involved in the practice of the traditional art of worship. They are unjustly described in many circles as witches and wizards, though they are only active in the pursuit of knowledge – a knowledge that can only be obtained through experience of ritual. They are mostly involved in the interpretation of the ancient ceremonies attributed to the Qabala, a Hebrew tradition that is believed by many to explain the whole of existence. The Golden Dawn itself was set up in London by its leader, a man by the name of Mathers. He has written the ceremonies that must be invoked in the progression through the various levels of the society. He is widely accredited to have made contact with 'the Secret Chiefs', who, to my limited understanding, are believed to be the Gods that hold all the answers to life on this planet. As a result of their teaching he set up the Golden Dawn.

"That is the story of the Golden Dawn, and how it came to be in existence. Now, there has been a considerable feud over the last few months between Mathers, who has moved to Germany, and those members of The Order he has left to run things here in London. This has resulted in Mathers demanding that the lodge be either disbanded completely, else all its possessions handed over to him. Hence that is the crux of the case. He has taken the Order to court, where I have been involved in defending them against his unlawful claims."

"That is some story," I said at the first chance, "So, Holmes, the missing accomplice in this case must be this chap Mathers?"

"Let us not rush to conclusions, Watson. From my enquiries yesterday, Mathers is still in Germany, which means he must have someone working for him. I think that is the man we are after," replied Holmes, "Tell me, Mr Gill, was it Mathers who made the original complaint to Scotland Yard?"

Mr Gill rummaged in his bag and withdrew a notebook and foolscap file. "I do not believe it was, Mr Holmes. No, here we are, the complaint was made by somebody of the name of Edward Aleister. Here, I have the original form from the police."

Holmes took the piece of paper offered him and studied it intently. Mr Gill and myself waited for his conclusion, both pleased that the sordid matter had come to what we thought to be its conclusion.

"I fear this signature to be forged, Mr Gill," said Holmes eventually.

"How can you tell?" he replied.

"I cannot be sure, it is only a first hypothesis. However, I have some idea as to who this mysterious person may be and his name is certainly not Edward Aleister. If you should like to observe, I can soon demonstrate the authenticity of the signature."

We followed Holmes as he rose and walked towards the chemicals he had been working on all afternoon. He decanted a small amount of blue liquid into a small saucer and delicately submerged the piece of paper. The ink began to fade slowly and, just as it was about to disappear completely, Holmes poured in a measured amount of opaquely green liquid. The paper was obscured from sight by the mixing of the two chemicals, so Holmes retrieved it with the aid of a pair of small tweezers and laid it on a surface to dry. Once it was in position, he took his magnifying glass from his pocket and began to study it. "Just as I thought," he mumbled as he straightened himself upright and handed me the glass.

I took the glass and looked at the paper, though was completely ignorant as to what a faded signature had to offer in way of a clue. "I cannot fathom what you are trying to get at, Holmes."

"Look at the signature, Watson. You will notice that I have succeeded in removing most of the ink, leaving only those patches where more ink was present."

"I still don't see what that means," I conceded.

"Why, it shows us that the name in the signature is not the same name as the man who put it on the paper. If I were to write my signature, the only places where there was a larger amount of ink would be at the top and bottom of strokes, and where the stroke of the nib has changed direction. For example, there would be more ink at the apex of a capital 'A' than there would in the middle of the stroke of a capital 'I'. In the last name of this signature, all the large patches of ink are in the correct place, at the top, bottom or point of change in the stroke, but in the first name, that of 'Edward', there are patches of ink where the stroke should have flowed. This proves that the man we are dealing with does not have the name of 'Edward', else his signature would be less patchy and the ink would not have disappeared from only these points here." Holmes used a small needle to point out patches of ink at the bottom of strokes. "But you notice that the ink has not been removed completely from these points." Again he pointed the needle at the middle of numerous upright strokes.

"Yes, I see what you are getting at, Holmes. If the person was fully confident in his own signature, he would not have stalled the movement of his pen, as is the case here," I said.

"Exactly, Watson."

"Why that is brilliant, Mr Holmes," exclaimed Mr Gill, "But why does the test not show up on the name 'Aleister'?"

"Because that is the man's real name, albeit his Christian and not his surname. It is quite simple really. I believe our mysterious man to be Aleister Crowley. You may remember, Watson, that we had an indirect dealing with him in the case of the Haunted House in Chancery Lane, last year."

I was about to congratulate my companion for his incredible display of intuition, but the door was flung open and a hoard of young street boys walked in, defying the protests of Mrs Hudson.

"Ah, Perkins," said Holmes to the tallest of the Baker Street Irregulars, "What news do you bring of the whereabouts of our friend, Aleister Crowley?"

"He has sailed for America, Mr Holmes," replied the boy promptly.

Once the Baker Street Irregulars had departed along with our guest Mr Gill, Holmes turned to me. "It is a great shame that our opponent has evaded us on this occasion, Watson, though he has certainly not gained anything from his considerable display of cunning. Although I have been outwitted on this occasion, I am sure that if we cross the path of his Scarlet Woman once more, I shall be more than prepared."

BOOK III

THE SCARLET WOMAN

CHAPTER ONE
A Vision

"And I am telling you, Watson, that if I am to take a pain killer, it may as well be from my own bottle," said Sherlock Holmes at my suggested prescription.

It was one of the coldest days London had ever known. The snow had fallen heavily over the streets some days previously and was now dangerously icy. Indeed many of the cab drivers had refused completely to ply for hire until the road gave them some semblance of grip. Sherlock Holmes was suffering an acute attack of rheumatism in his wrist and had kept it to himself for some weeks. It was plainly evident that he was in considerable pain for he winced at the lifting of even the smallest object. It had come to the point where I could respect the man's pride no longer and had to step in by offering a compound to ease the stiffness. His pride was nothing compared to his stubbornness, however, and he was refusing my medical advice, preferring to rely on his wretched syringe and eight percent solution.

"Holmes, you really are one of the most obstinate specimens I have ever had to deal with," I conceded when my resolve had been eroded. I looked at his thin frame. Rheumatism was a common enough ailment in someone with such awkward bone structure. The thinness of his limbs and his gaunt features were ideal for a touch of rheumatism and, given the extreme chill, Holmes did not help himself to any extent by insisting on walking the streets in the course of the one or two cases he was currently working on. I sighed loudly in protest as he stalked across the room in search of the small leather case which contained his syringe and bottle of cocaine. He became more agitated as he threw papers from side to side in his search, his untidiness finally becoming too much even for him.

My smile faded when he finally located the leather case, but, before he had time to unbutton it, his attention was diverted. His tall frame stood to attention as he picked out the sound of the door being closed downstairs and the light steps of our landlady, Mrs Hudson, ascending the stairs. She opened the door, entered and was startled by Holmes's sudden question:

"Who is it?" he cried, "And what is his business?"

"Mr Holmes, you are the most impatient of men," replied Mrs Hudson, through one of her understanding smiles, "Why should it necessarily be a visitor?"

"And how do you know that it is not a woman?" I said suddenly.

Mrs Hudson went to explain who it was, but Holmes held a hand up to stop her. "No, don't tell me, my good Mrs Hudson. There is surely a visitor, for the door was held open too long for just one person to enter. I suggest our visitor was about to ring on the bell when Mrs Hudson here returned from her trip to the grocers. She opened the door for him and then they both entered, hence the unusual length of opening. And surely, Watson, even you must have noticed that no cab pulled up in the street. If it was a woman, she would have taken a cab, so it is an easy deduction that our visitor is a man. I would like to make one further point, that is that our visitor is a polite, somewhat meek man of not more than forty years."

"And how the devil can you make such a guess?" I said.

"Guess, Watson? I am not in the business of guessing, but I did notice that the door was not closed by Mrs Hudson. It did not slam shut as would be normal, but was shut slowly and carefully. Only a meek man would take such care. I would suggest him to be under the age of forty, for any man over that age would have been in the normal habit of waiting for the housekeeper to shut the door before she offered to take his coat."

"You and your games, Mr Holmes. You are correct in every detail, would you now care for me to send him up?" replied Mrs Hudson, throwing a slight wink in my direction.

"Did he give a name?" I asked.

"No, he refused. But maybe Mr Holmes would be as good as to tell us."

"My dear Mrs Hudson, I feel that is too much for even my powers of deduction," replied Holmes quickly, with a fond twinkle in his eye, "But if you would be good enough to show him up, we shall know soon enough."

"Surely it is a case that beckons us, Holmes?" I said when Mrs Hudson had departed.

"Indeed it must be, Watson, for nothing that was not urgent would bring a man out in such horrid weather as this."

Holmes sat in his chair and drew his tobacco slipper from the floor in front of the warm hearth. There was hardly a sound from the steps on the stair and the door was opened with either fear or a severe case of shyness. A man hesitated on the verge of the room, prompted forward by Holmes's remark that he should not allow the heat to escape on such a cold day. He took two paces in whereupon he was open to both our inquisitive stares. He was indeed of the age Holmes had placed him at, being to my mind in his mid thirties. He was of slight stature and his seemingly nervous disposition made him stoop slightly, with his hat clenched in front of him. His overcoat was untidy and somewhat unfashionable and he had a shock of untidy graying hair. When he lifted his head, it was easy to see that he was a very handsome man. His forehead was high and his chin was squarely set, though not overbearing. His beautifully proportioned nose supported a pair of rounded prince nez.

"Pray come and sit in this chair, my good Sir. You must surely be cold, come warm yourself by the fire before you tell me how I can be of assistance. Dr Watson will take your coat," said Holmes warmly.

I stood and removed the coat from the reluctant visitor and ushered him to the spare chair. He sat and rubbed his hands enthusiastically towards the warm flames of our substantial fire. Holmes leant back and lit his pipe while casting an interested eye over our mysterious arrival. Eventually the man spoke.

"The strange event I have to tell you may seem somewhat fantastical but to be sure it is true, if not now, then at some point in the nearest of futures," said the man in a quiet voice in some accent I could not quite place.

"Tell me sir, do you write upon your own country? I speak of course of that country that has produced some of the greatest works of literature – Ireland," replied Holmes.

"Then you have heard of me, no doubt," replied the man as his mouth broadened into a genial smile.

"I have no prior knowledge of you in the slightest," replied Holmes quickly. "Your accent is well disguised but your construction of sentences is both of that type used by Irish people and, if I may say, the lyricism of the poet. You have introduced yourself in a way which arouses curiosity rather than the more obvious cold tone of straight forward explanation. The slight ink mark on the middle finger of your right hand shows you to be an habitual writer. Coupled with the slight swelling under that ink mark I would suggest you have written for a prolonged period. I should not have been so bold as to suggest this written word was any more than a clerk would be used to, but on entering this room, you studied intently all its features while you were warming your hands. No doubt you could already construct a somewhat fanciful passage on our humble abode. And then of course there is the thickness of your spectacles, they give away your scholarly pursuits. They are surely too strong for every day activities, but essential for reading. You have travelled some distance this cold morning, with reading glasses. Consequently, it is not more than an obvious deduction that reading takes up considerable time in your life. You are not a rich man, for you have had a long journey this morning and a man of more means than yourself would surely take a cab. I realise that the pursuit of money for such a learned man as yourself would not be difficult if you were so inclined. And a most admirable course of action that is, not unlike my own."

"I had been warned of your ability, Mr Holmes," said the man suddenly, "But it is still something that cannot be fully appreciated without the good fortune of hearing it at first hand."

"I am as committed to my science as you are to your art, but please tell me your name and what it is that weighs on you."

"My name is Yeats, William Butler Yeats."

"W.B. Yeats?" I cried suddenly.

"So you have heard of me, Dr Watson," he said quickly.

"But of course. You are a poet whose reputation is growing. I have read some of your work though I do confess to preferring the poetry over some of your prose. I was not a great admirer of 'The Countess Cathleen'."

"Ah, now you would not have been alone there, Dr Watson, it was not favoured by many of my fellow countrymen either. Indeed, some even went as far as calling it blasphemous," he replied in good humour.

"Tell me of your religion, Mr Yeats," Holmes suddenly cut in.

"My religion? I should think a man's religion to be his own worry," came the sharp reply.

"As you wish," said Holmes, "if Watson has finished his praise for your written word, then maybe it is time to get down to the business of your visit. I am a very busy man and I am sure you also have little time to waste."

"Indeed, Mr Holmes," sulked Yeats, still somewhat shocked at the briskness of Holmes's question of religion, "Though I am not sure you will be of any help. I have an interest in matters of the spirit and what I hold to be something of meaning a pragmatic man – like yourself – will surely shrug off as weak superstition. I implore you to give me a fair hearing though, as this matter will surely stimulate your imagination."

"Please proceed."

"You are a man of considerable intelligence, Mr Holmes, and possibly the only person who could investigate this strange event. I have called on you because I will get nowhere with the police. For one reason or another, although I have more respect for them than my fellow countrymen, they will not give me a fair hearing and I am sure that they would never believe what I am about to tell you."

Yeats's voice had grown even weaker than was natural and he had leaned forward with pleading eyes. Holmes studied his face intently and grasped his long chin with his fingertips in anticipation. "I must say, Mr Yeats, that I experience the same apprehension in my numerous dealings with Scotland Yard."

"I have already said that I am a very spiritual man, Mr Holmes, perhaps more so than could ever be understood by those who are not privy to my most private of activities. I frequently have visions, indeed I am often instrumental in invoking them in the first instance. It is a necessary part of my writing, and of self-fulfilment. Many cynical men may call them dreams or even apparitions, but I implore you to believe me when I say that there have been several occasions when my visions have manifested themselves materially. Although last night's vision came to me in my sleep, I know my conscious mind to have been fully awake and riding on the vision like the full moon would ride its reflection on the crest of a wave. Every ghastly image of that vision I know to be true. Whether it has at this point in time come to fruition, I have no way of knowing, but if it has not thus far, it most certainly will."

"Then you must tell us of this vision, Mr Yeats, and be sure not to leave out even the smallest detail."

I looked up at Holmes with a certain amount of surprise that he had not dismissed our visitor's obvious eccentricity. It was not in Holmes's nature to listen to 'psychic' perceptions which could never be proved material. Indeed, I have often remarked that my friend knew little of metaphysics, in the main this was because there could be no proof of such theories and hence he would not spend time on them.

"It is quite the most horrible image I have ever had conjured up in my mind," continued Yeats, "And I assure you here and now that this image was not invoked by myself, but put into my mind by the spiritual disturbance the incident has created."

"Ah, so you say the incident had occurred," interrupted Holmes quickly, "But perhaps you will say you know not whether it has, and that it may well be possible for it to occur at some point in the future."

"I am practical to a point, Mr Holmes, and I realise that the incident has probably not occurred yet because surely if it had, the papers would be full of it. All I am saying is that in the vision, it most definitely had occurred. If you understand that time is not necessarily linear, you would believe me when I say that a vision allows you to look on an event as if it had happened, but in effect you are looking to some future time. I know this event to have happened, but I cannot tell you when it will, or whether it has actually occurred."

"I am not of the same mind as you, Mr Yeats, and do not subscribe to psychic perception, but please continue with the specifics of what you have seen."

"The vision I have seen is not for the faint-hearted, of that you must be sure. I had fallen asleep last night in not the warmest of rooms, but what came to my mind in the night left me with a severe fever. I was taken from my own body by a spirit that I have known for some time. The spirit in question acted as a guide as it led me through the dark streets of one of the most dangerous parts of this city. We came to a halt outside of a dark alley, a deserted alley that led to a bleak courtyard. I could feel the cold cobbles through my bare foot and was shivering beyond my own control, but what I was shown to was enough to send me to fever. In the corner of the yard, I could just make out an object hidden behind a piece of timber. My guiding spirit urged me to turn the piece of wood over and so I did. There, in front of my very eyes, beating in the snow was a heart. A naked heart cut from some living body, the blood was streaming from its dying vessels and seeped into the snow it was rested in. As I looked on in horror, I could see the life disappearing from it, and then I noticed on the under side what had caused it to die. There was a twisted dagger plunged into its centre. I could only see the black handle, though presumed the sharp blade to have been thrust in with some force. It was more than I could take. Never before have I seen something so gruesome, it had an immediate effect and I was suddenly awake in my bed, screaming.

"I knew not what to do, Mr Holmes. I assure you that I am of my full senses and this was as real as if I had been awake through the entire incident. I looked upon the soles of my feet and found them to be covered in chilblains, as if I had walked outside bare-footed. It has turned my stomach and I will never be able to rest easy until someone has gotten to the bottom of this queer happening."

There was no doubt about his sincerity. He believed in what he had seen but I had little sympathy for him. I did not believe a word of what he had said – recognising the symptoms of fairly advanced paranoia. He shook and his eyes had the dark fear etched into their very make-up, it was an easy case for a medic to diagnose – he had lost his senses completely and the case in front of us had little to do with crime, but rather what had led this poor man to be so fearful. But if I had a psychological solution to the problem, to my surprise, the story seemed to catch the imagination of Sherlock Holmes.

"Sleep walking is a common complaint enough in our city today, Mr Yeats. Maybe Dr Watson would be a better judge of what has occurred, but have you ever before found yourself waking in a place away from where you fell asleep?"

"Never, Mr Holmes. I realise that my story may verge on the fantastical, but to me it is real enough," replied Yeats quickly.

"Ah, that's as maybe, Mr Yeats, but I really cannot see how we are to be of assistance to you."

"I was hoping that with an investigation, you could perhaps find that this vision is actually real and that somewhere there is a heart with a dagger plunged into it."

"Did you recognise the courtyard in which you saw the heart?"

"No I did not, there was no sign that was sharp enough to read and even the immediate walls were too blurred to allow me to guess at where they may be."

"But you said that your spirit guided you through the streets of London, surely you could recognise the route and lead us to it."

"If only it was so, Mr Holmes. As I say, it was dream-like, and as such there was no real way of trying to get any sort of bearing."

"Then there is nothing we can do for you. The only course of action would be to search every courtyard in London which would be beyond our modest resources. I am afraid that I cannot help you."

"I can understand how it must seem, Mr Holmes, and I respect the fact that you cannot work on something of which you clearly have no knowledge. I am sorry, Gentlemen, that I have wasted your time," replied our visitor.

Yeats stood as if to leave, but hovered for some time once his coat was around his neck. I shuffled uncomfortably at his continued presence and noticed that Holmes had lost himself in thought. Eventually, after a clear minute had elapsed, Yeats disappeared through the door without another word.

"I have never known such a queer tale, Holmes," I said at last, "He must surely be mad to think that we would believe a word of what he has told us. I must say that he would be an excellent case for some of those new French psychologists."

"Indeed you may be right, Watson. However, it is not so uncommon for a criminal to verge on the insane and allow himself to get caught, as if it were a game. There is something to what our visitor told us, of that I am sure, though it is surely more sinister than a mere dream."

"Then you believe him, Holmes?"

"I believe merely that somewhere in London we may well find some atrocity as he has described to us. But I also believe that the only person who could have committed the atrocity would be the only person with knowledge of it."

"Then you are saying that Yeats is telling you that he has, or at least plans to commit a crime involving a live heart."

"Indeed, it seems a most likely conclusion, Watson. But there is nothing that can be done about it now. I would expect Scotland Yard to think us as odd as we thought him, if we should recount the tale to them. It may come to nothing, but I suggest this case will develop before our very eyes."

I found it difficult to share Holmes's hopes for the case, but was surprised when a couple of days later we should have a report of an incident similar in every detail to that which Yeats had foretold.

CHAPTER TWO
A Diabolical Discovery

"Ah, Lestrade," cried Holmes, as the Inspector stalked quickly into the room. Holmes had been flicking through the morning's paper with the agitation that is only brought about through boredom. His eyes lit up considerably at the unexpected visit of Scotland Yard's famous detective, as it meant a consultation was on hand. "Please tell me you have come to engage me in an incident that is of sufficient gravity to warrant my opinion."

"I must say, Holmes, that it is not my idea to consult you, but even I have to follow orders from above."

"You have not found religion, have you Lestrade?" replied Holmes, wickedly.

"I should rather think your sense of humour as somewhat misplaced since we are dealing with the return of Jack The Ripper."

"Jack the Ripper!" I spluttered.

"Impossible," replied Holmes calmly, dismissively.

"Ah, now that is exactly what my superior said, Mr Holmes. His exact words were, 'It is impossible that Jack the Ripper has returned. Consult Sherlock Holmes and he will prove to you that Jack the Ripper is no longer any concern to us.' I must say that I do not share your optimism."

"So you have a victim then? A murder that has been committed in the style of Jack the Ripper?"

"Not yet, Mr Holmes, but it will only take time, you mark my words."

"Then, perhaps you would be good enough to explain to me what exactly you have got by way of evidence," replied Holmes calmly.

"The evidence we have is not for the faint hearted, it is enough to give even the most hardened of my men nightmares. A prostitute, by the name of Anna Giles, has been reported missing from the East End. No trace of her can be found, all her belongings remain in her room. This is not out of the usual but, linked with this morning's developments, it has become more sinister. As you will recall, in the case of Jack the Ripper, his last two victims were both killed within six hundred yards of each other. In the early hours of this morning we were called to a most gruesome discovery at the site of the murder of his fifth victim, namely Mary Jane Kelly outside of the house in which she boarded in Dorset Street. A member of the public had been clearing away some refuse from the street when he uncovered a single heart, its blood frozen into the icy snow. This, you may think is bad enough, that a man should unwittingly stumble across a heart that has been cut from a living animal, but the worst is yet to come. Not only was there this fresh heart, but it had a small dagger plunged into it up to the hilt."

I let out a gasp and looked across at Holmes who had obviously had the same thought as myself. "This is not the work of Jack the Ripper, Inspector, of that you may take my word."

"Ah, but that is not all, Holmes, for the connection was not made from this discovery alone. Only a matter of hours after we were confronted with this terrible act were we called to Mitre Square where some workmen had started their day. They had lifted some timber that was to be used in the building works only to discover a heart. It was exactly the same as the one found earlier and also had a dagger plunged into its centre, from the underside. It was only when one of the older officers remembered being called to the Ripper murders on exactly the same spot, that we realised what we had on our hands."

"Presumably you have investigated the sites of the other three Ripper murders?" asked Holmes.

"On realising the gravity of these two gruesome discoveries, I reported it to my superior at once. He was, as I have said, of the opinion it was not Jack the Ripper and ordered me here to Baker Street. I have carried out his order in consulting you, Mr Holmes, though I do think this is a matter for the police and do not see how you can be of any assistance. We have dispatched a team to each of the other murder sites and I am hoping for a report from them shortly. I have now carried out my order and informed you of the case. I shall take my leave, as I have a lot of work ahead of me."

"Then we shall accompany you, Lestrade. Come along Watson," said Holmes reaching for his cape.

"You will do no such thing, Mr Holmes. I have told you this is a police matter and you would be well advised to stay out of the way. I have fulfilled the order to inform you, and that is all there is to do. I shall afford you no chance to continue this investigation while I have all the theories I need," replied Lestrade angrily.

"You can have all the theories you like, Lestrade. So far they are all wrong, as even Watson here must know. And as for your refusal to allow me to accompany you, I am sure a quick telegram to your superior will do the trick."

Lestrade's eyes flashed in anger at the threat of Holmes informing his superior, but he knew there was little he could do. "Very well, Holmes, you may accompany us back to Mitre Square, though I assure you that you are wasting your time. This is not a case for an amateur."

Not one word was spoken in our journey into the East End of London. Holmes was lost in his own thoughts and Lestrade was angrily sulking from being forced to take us with him to Mitre Square. The newly settled snow was hazardous in the extreme, having drifted into huge piles on both sides of the roads. The main thoroughfares of Fenchurch Street and Aldgate were not so hazardous that we could not navigate our way around the more icy patches, but when we drew up along Mitre Street, the snow was too thick for us to pass. We left the cab and made the last hundred yards or so of our journey on foot, and turned into a dark passageway.

"Lestrade, one moment please," shouted Holmes at the rapidly disappearing figure in front of us.

Lestrade stopped in his tracks and turned around slowly, somewhat annoyed at having been interrupted. "Yes, what is it, Mr Holmes?"

"You have not told us about the hearts themselves, Lestrade. Are they human?"

"Ah, I am not a medical man, Mr Holmes, and I really could not give you an answer. We have sent down to Scotland Yard for a medic, but he had not arrived by the time I left to come to you. I dare say he will be here by now."

When we reached the end of the small passage, it opened up into a gloomy courtyard. This was Mitre Square, a large area with houses built up high three sides, the cobbled floor was covered with snow which stretched for three sides of the square. The fourth side had been protected by an overhanging roof and was not covered in snow, but had the sheen of glassy ice. To one side of the square was St. James's church, and it was on this side that a huddle of policemen were stooping over to examine what looked like a pile of timber.

"I see the press have not caught wind of this yet, Lestrade," I said, looking at the local people who were asking the statue-like policemen questions for which there was no answer.

"Indeed they have not, Dr Watson. I dare say we will not be able to keep it quiet for long, but the last thing we need is for the papers to whip up that hysteria that got in the way of our investigation of the original Ripper cases."

Holmes was quiet. He had come to a halt in the centre of the square and was casting his eye around the buildings that were throwing shadows all around us. While Lestrade and I made our way to the scene of the crime, Holmes took a brisk walk around the perimeter of the square before rejoining us. The small cordon of policemen opened up to let us through. On the floor was a huge pile of timber. The large pieces, that were no doubt to be used as supports in the building work in an adjacent site to our left, had been cleared in the centre and there, set into a pile of snow was the object that had given so much horror to those that had been privy to it. It was a heart, of that there was little doubt, but it was set into the snow and frozen so that its shape was contorted away from the natural. Spreading out in little streams all around it was blood. It had run for not more than four inches before its trace was frozen into the snow.

"Well, Dr Watson, what do you make of it?" asked Lestrade.

"It is one of the most horrible things I have ever seen in my life, Inspector, most horrible."

"Well, it appears that our medical man has not been able to get here as yet," continued Lestrade.

"But it is not human is it, Watson?" said Holmes suddenly, from behind us.

"No it is not," I replied, "It has been frozen into a most unusual shape, but it is too small to be of human origin."

"That hardly bodes well for your hypothesis that the Ripper is back, is that not so, Lestrade?" taunted Holmes.

"You may go your own way on this, Holmes, but the coincidence is too much – you seem to be forgetting the disappearance of Anna Giles. Indeed, this spot is the exact spot that the victim of the Ripper was found. I hardly think it could be a copy murder when that information was not made available to the public. There are very few people who know the exact facts of that case, but one of which was surely the murderer himself, Jack the Ripper," replied Lestrade.

"Has it been moved?" asked Holmes.

"It has been turned once and put back exactly in place. That is how we know there is a small dagger plunged into its underside. The heart found in Dorset Street has already been taken to the Yard for a thorough examination."

"Well, Watson, this is certainly within your realm. Perhaps you would be good enough to conduct a quick examination and give me your conclusions."

With some apprehension, both on my own part and that of Lestrade, I bent towards the floor and removed my gloves. I gently picked the heart up, feeling the extreme cold through my bones. It was rigid and, on turning it over, fitted snugly in the palm of my hand. But it was not the heart itself that gave me such revulsion, it was what had been placed into the heart. There, on the underside, was a small dagger, not more than six inches in length. The blade had been embedded in the frozen flesh, but the handle was fully visible. It was made of a dark wood, possibly stained to make it close to black in colour and was decorated with various symbols that made no sense to me, but seemed somehow sinister. Perched on top of the handle was a small, carved, ivory skull.

"Well, Watson, what are your conclusions?" said Holmes suddenly. He leant in towards me, so he was closer to the object I held outstretched in my hand.

"It is not human, Holmes, I would suggest it to have come from a small animal, most probably a pig, but it could be a small sheep. Whoever has cut it out, knows little of what they were doing. They have used a blunt instrument and have hacked rather than cut. If you look at the aorta, you can see that it has not been cut at all, but ripped from the body."

Holmes did not reply. Instead, he took his magnifying glass from a pocket in his cloak and examined the heart in the minutest detail. Occasionally, he would let out a short sound as if he had stumbled across something, but he gave no explanation. By the time he had finished, my hand was numb and I had trouble replacing the heart back in the small hole in the snow.

"Well, what do you make of it, Holmes?" At hearing my question, Lestrade, who had wandered across to give his men some orders as to what they should say to the crowd of inquisitive locals that were amassing in greater numbers, walked back towards us.

"It is, as you say, not a human heart, Watson. But there are some very singular details about it. It has been cut from the body of its victim, not in any unskilled way, as you suppose but, rather, in a stupendous hurry. The ripping of the aorta is somewhat surprising, though I think our man has probably panicked and, instead of taking the time to cut, has resorted to brute strength. It is not necessarily a blunt instrument that they have used. They have hacked, but if you look closely at the lines of cut flesh, you will notice the clear markings of a serrated knife. The serrated edge is on the left-hand side of the blade, and as such is not an easy tool for a left-handed person to use, hence the appearance of rather an unskilled job. We know the man to be left-handed, because of the angle of the cuts into the main arteries. How long do you suppose the heart has been out of the body?"

"It is difficult to say, Holmes. It has been frozen, so there is little I can do to guess at how long it has been there. It was fresh when placed in the snow, of that I am certain, for there is blood running a trace from the heart through the snow, but it could have been there from the first snowfall. It has been preserved exactly."

"Yes, that may well be the case, Watson. But I have asked the workmen if they were working yesterday. They replied in the affirmative and, further, that the timber was only delivered yesterday afternoon. It would seem strange for them not to discover the heart then, would it not? So I presume it to have been left here at some point during the night."

Holmes bent down and, with some difficulty, managed to pull the dagger from the flesh it had been frozen into. He stood up straight and examined the blade. "This is not the knife that was used to cut the heart from the body and, what is more, the knife was placed into the heart after it had been removed from the body. There is no blood on the handle. If the knife had been plunged in while the heart was still beating, or was at least still full of blood, you would expect some of the blood to fly up the handle."

"Yes, that is true, Holmes," I replied, "Though you must admit that we have a suspect already?" I said the last words in a whisper so that they could not be overheard by Lestrade or any of the officers who had set about marking the pieces of timber.

"This is a most interesting case, Watson, and one that I should much like to discuss with you when we are away from the cold. The amount of activity here has, as ever with the police wading in head first, distorted any chance of finding prints or other such clues," replied Holmes. "Here one moment, Lestrade – Please!"

"Yes, Holmes. What is it?" said the Inspector, annoyed at his attention being distracted.

"I would be much obliged if you would allow me to keep possession of this dagger. I need to make a full examination of it back at Baker Street. You have one that is similar from the other heart in Dorset Street, and I assure you that you shall be the first to know of any developments that come from this examination."

"As you wish, Holmes, though I shall have to pick it up later this evening, so make your examination quickly."

"Good, then we shall meet later this evening, Lestrade."

"But do we not want to visit the site of the other incident?" I asked Holmes as we made our way back to Aldgate.

"It is a matter of priority, Watson. I feel we can gain more from a thorough examination of the facts of this singular incident than clouding the issue with an examination of Dorset Street. There will be no more clues there, of that I am sure. The man who has committed this deed has been very methodical and has left little by way of evidence as to his identity. If I recall the investigation into Jack the

Ripper, Dorset Street, although a narrow and by no means main road, is in constant use by the local residents. That was one of the reasons that the murder of Mary Kelly took place inside and not outside like the other four murders. Any clue that may have existed will have long since been destroyed in the few hours of this morning. If the need arises, we can visit Dorset Street at some later time, but at the present, we need to make some positive headway while the trail is still warm."

CHAPTER THREE
The Return Of Aleister Crowley

While I was removing my outer garments in the front room of our apartment in Baker Street and pushing my hands towards the fire for some gratefully appreciated warmth, Holmes had left the room and I could hear the front door slam behind him. He returned within ten minutes with the nervous enthusiasm that only came when he felt an especial challenge in a case.

"Holmes," I said. He had sat next to the fire and was sucking on his strong tobacco as he examined the small dagger that was being flicked through all angles in the palm of his hand, "Surely you have made the same connection that I have and that the answer to this mystery lies in the visit of Yeats."

"Indeed, Watson, a most unlikely coincidence I would agree, but tell me, in your mind, do you think Mr Yeats to have been responsible for these most disturbing incidents? Did he strike you as the type to be cavorting with prostitutes?"

"I do not know of prostitutes, Holmes, but he came and told you of his intentions. All the rubbish he spoke of visions was merely a blind, so that he could tell you his intended course of action, last night."

"Would it put your mind at rest if I told you that I have sent the Baker Street Irregulars to summon him to our apartment without delay?"

"Indeed it would, Holmes, for he must hold the key to this extraordinary case."

"He may well hold the key, Watson, but he was not the person responsible for the planting of those two hearts."

"How can you be sure of that, Holmes? How else would he have been able to predict this queer crime?"

"Well, as I explained to you, the man who perpetrated this ghastly incident, was left handed. That much was obvious from the cuts in the flesh. But your foremost suspect, Yeats, is right-handed. I know that because I remarked on the ink stain that was on his middle finger. Now what man would use a knife in the opposite hand to that which was most natural? We may conclude that Mr Yeats did not perpetrate the deed. As to how he managed to predict the police discovery, for he did predict, given that the hearts could not have been placed in the snow at any time before yesterday evening – that is still a mystery but one that we shall solve, Watson."

"Have you any other hypotheses then, Holmes?"

"Many as yet, Watson, though I know not which one will fit the case that will open up before us. We need more to work on. At the moment, all I know of the culprit for certain is that he is a small but strong man, in possession of a pair of leather gloves."

"You have lost me in your deductions yet again, Holmes," I conceded.

"It is fairly logical, I assure you. It takes some force to be able to plunge a knife into such tough flesh as is found in the heart. Now the handle of this knife is no longer than three inches. It may have been possible for pressure to have been exerted on the top of the handle, by pushing down on the skull carving, but that would not have resulted in such a clean hole in which the blade slid. No, the man who pushed this blade in, held it firmly around the handle and plunged it in for all his strength. To get a grip on the handle, the man must surely have a smaller hand than either you or I, Watson. Although it is not always the case, a small hand is not found on a large man, hence I deduce our man to be not more than five and a half feet tall."

"And where do the leather gloves come in?"

"Well, if we examine the handle of the knife closely, there are only one set of fingerprints, and those I can identify straight away as yours. Now this should strike you as odd should it not? For even if our suspect had not handled the knife personally then you would expect some fingerprints somewhere, even if it was only from the person who sold him the knives. But there were no fingerprints until the time the heart was discovered, when you took it into your own hand. I have conducted a study on the most effective material for cleaning away that layer of grease that makes up a fingerprint and found that leather was considerably better than any other material you would be able to make a pair of gloves from."

"It could be that he cleaned the knife before he put the gloves on, Holmes."

"Indeed, that had crossed my mind also. But there are rough edges to the symbols cut into this knife's handle. I can think of only a pair of good quality leather gloves that would not leave some strand of material on one of those edges. For example, wool would have surely left even the most minute trace snagged on an edge. You see, Watson, that it is often as much help to notice the absence of something as it is to make some material discovery."

These were the final words to come from Sherlock Holmes for two hours. During that time, he sat in the chair, occasionally restocking his pipe, but all the while looking at the dagger he turned over and over in his hand. I busied myself with trying to rearrange my notes of the case thus far. I occasionally looked out of the window to see if the snow had stopped falling, for I had run out of my brand of tobacco and felt in need of a brisk afternoon walk. Alas, it was not to be, for the snow was falling thicker than ever. But even with this blizzard blowing outside, I was surprised to hear the front door slam shut below us.

Holmes jumped from his seat as though he had been violently woken. He had heard the sound and moved rapidly to the door. He stretched out his arm and pulled the door open just as Perkins was about to make his entrance. I could see the expression on Holmes's face drop as he realised the visitor was not whom he was expecting.

"Mr Holmes, Sir," began the street urchin. But before he could finish his introduction, Yeats stepped from the top of the stairs and proceeded towards Holmes.

"Ah, Mr Yeats, for one moment then I thought my little army of youth here had failed in their quest to find your whereabouts, either that or you had refused to come," said Holmes, "Here Perkins, a sovereign for yourself and five crowns to be shared amongst your ranks."

"Thank you kindly, Sir," replied the boy, snatching the money from the hand of Holmes and disappearing down the stairs before any of us had time to blink.

"A most efficient workforce you have at your disposal, Mr Holmes," said Yeats as he removed his coat and handed it to me.

"Indeed, they have been most valuable to me," replied Holmes, quickly ushering Yeats to the spare chair.

I ordered some tea from Mrs Hudson, by leaning over the top banister and shouting down before I returned to the room and quickly took my position in the vacant seat.

".......must be some reason why you should care to be understanding as to my position," Yeats was saying as I sat down.

"And there is, Mr Yeats. You are an intelligent man, and I think you know as well as I why I have summoned you here, though I admit that I had not expected you to come in good humour."

"I do not come in good humour, Mr Holmes," Yeats replied, "I am just pleased, in a way, that what I told you yesterday has indeed materialised. You see, that shows you that what I said yesterday was true and that I am not as mad as you must have thought when I left this house."

"Then you know about the two hearts that were discovered at this morning's earliest hour?"

"Two?" said Yeats, in a shocked tone, "I only imagined there to be one."

"Imagined or knew?" asked Holmes sharply.

"Imagined, I suppose," said Yeats in an absent way. He sat for some moments in silence, his eyes lost in the leaping flames of the fire. Suddenly, he recovered himself, when he said, "What do you mean, 'imagined or knew'? I do not understand your question, nor do I care for its tone."

"I am sure you do not, Mr Yeats. I realise you were not the perpetrator of this little incident, but you have, by your own definition, knowledge of the deed. Henceforth, you must presumably know both who the perpetrator is and also what the meaning is behind it. Perhaps......"

But Holmes's sentence was cut off by the arrival of the tea, brought in on the solid silver salver that is normally only used when one of my companion's more illustrious clients was in attendance. The silver had only been seen by a select few which had included the Prime Minister, Home Secretary and future King of Bohemia. Mrs Hudson's action had not only been noticed by myself however, for I saw Holmes send her an enquiring look. She did not respond, for her eyes were firmly set on our visitor and I was in fear of her dropping the tray completely. As I stood to take her luggage from her, she smiled at Yeats, who had turned a rather startling shade of scarlet.

"I hope you do not mind, Sir," she suddenly said when I had relieved her of the tray and set it safely onto the table. Her eyes were set full on Yeats and he was beginning to shuffle uneasily in his chair. "I had not realised whom I had the pleasure of addressing yesterday. I am a great admirer of your works, though I am sure you are always being pestered by admirers."

"Um, not at all."

Holmes's face melted to an expression of amusement. He leant back and let a brief smile spread across his granite features at Mrs Hudson's performance. "Perhaps you would be so good as to tell us all about our guest?" said Holmes suddenly to Mrs Hudson, who looked up in shock, as if she had not realised our presence in the room.

"Mr Yeats here is one of our best poets, Mr Holmes. Why surely you have heard of his verse?"

"I must admit that I have not. I have little interest in idle romanticism."

"Then perhaps Mr Yeats would be so good as to recite some verses so you may base your opinions on fact and not imagination," replied our landlady undaunted.

"Very well," said Holmes in a most amused tone, "Maybe you would care to enlighten my ignorance."

"I am not sure this is appropriate, now," replied Yeats, completely embarrassed by the sudden turn of events.

"Please do," I urged, being caught in the enthusiasm for hearing some of the words from the man himself.

"Very well," he said. He began to recite in a voice that can only be described as magical. So soft, yet with command that had us all captured for the briefest of moments. His poem echoed beautifully through the room, provoking images of red, proud and sad roses.

I quite fancy that Mrs Hudson had a tear in her eye as Yeats finished his third stanza.

"I am sorry to have been such an imposition on your company. Please do not think badly of me. Your words have that Celtic spirit that is alive in all of us," said Mrs Hudson quickly. She then left us. I looked across at Holmes, who had a rather bemused look about him, and then to Yeats who had lost himself in thoughts of his own.

"You must excuse that unfortunate interruption, Mr Yeats. I should like to continue with the interview."

"Yes, of course."

"As I had been saying, you are surely aware of the meaning behind the two hearts, and the daggers that were found embedded in them."

"I know only what I had explained to you yesterday, Mr Holmes. It is that simple and, though you are loath to believe me, for I can see that in both your own and Dr Watson's face, all I know is what came to me in my vision of the heart and the dagger."

"But you do know where the heart was placed, is that not so?"

"As I have already explained, I could not make out the place, it was not familiar to me in the least. As for the reason behind the strange event, I can only offer you guesses. I have no knowledge of the reason nor of the perpetrator."

"We are going to have to take your word for this, Mr Yeats, though I should warn you that the police are now involved and that they would not accept your explanation."

"I quite understand that, Mr Holmes, and feel sure that the police would see me safely in an asylum rather than believe my explanation. I approached you because I have been assured that you are a man of the utmost discretion, and hold the police in as much distrust as I myself do," replied Yeats.

Holmes kept his eyes on the man. "Very well, Mr Yeats, we shall do nothing but accept your account as it stands at this moment. Now, perhaps you would be so good as to explain your own understanding of the case. I have laid the facts out in front of you, in the shape of the two most disturbing discoveries this morning, and would welcome your opinion."

"All I have to say on this matter is confidential, for the forces we are dealing with are not those that can be taken lightly," said Yeats, with the look of a frightened man.

"Our discretion is assured, Mr Yeats, please proceed."

"Well, in occult circles the heart is a most powerful symbol. It is the life of an object in the same way that a doctor will tell you it is at the centre of the human body. What we have here is a preparation for an occult ritual, a ritual that is to be of the most powerful influence, of that I am sure, for the symbols that are used are reserved only for the highest of adepts. It may well be that the person we are dealing with is a fraud, but I think not. Rather, they are someone who knows exactly what they are doing. The choice of the dagger is indicative of a rebirth. Rebirth can only come about with death. To invoke a spirit, there has to be a balance, there cannot be birth without death. The symbol of death is the dagger."

"So we are dealing with black magic?" I said, uneasy at the words I was hearing. Although I do not believe in magic, there is something daunting about those who do.

"Ah, now that is a common misconception, Dr Watson," replied Yeats, "Peddled, no doubt, by those who are accustomed to mocking that which they do not understand. There is no black or white magic, as defined so rigidly, for every action is subjective and the thin line between good and bad will be different for every man on this planet. In essence, Demon Est Deus Reversi – The Devil is merely the reverse side of God."

"Please, Yeats, Stop! You must explain to me what you mean by that," cried Holmes suddenly.

"Why nothing at all, merely trying to depict my explanation," returned Yeats, somewhat bemused.

"Come now, Man! I have heard the expression before. Perhaps you would care to tell me what you know of the Golden Dawn."

"What business is the Golden Dawn to you, Mr Holmes?"

"It has been at the centre of one of my previous investigations. It has not been beyond the influence of those who have nothing but the most evil intentions in mind."

"Why, that is slander, Sir!" cried Yeats.

"Well, I think we can take that as conclusive proof that you are a member of the society," replied Holmes calmly.

"Yes, I will admit that I am a member, but also that all you say is nothing of the true nature of our Order."

"What you have just quoted us, Mr Yeats, is a phrase that has been used in the past by a man called Aleister Crowley – do you know him?"

"Why, of course I do, but if your knowledge is that thorough then you must surely know that he is no longer a member of the Order. As I have already explained, occultism and the study of inner knowledge is only possible through the rebirth of an adept and, as such, it is common practice within an order to be reborn once you have reached a certain degree. This process can be accompanied by changing the name by which you are known to other initiates. Demon Est Deus Reversi is the name I have been born into by the Golden Dawn. Aleister Crowley, in the course of his argument with the Golden Dawn that eventually led to his expulsion, used to his own ends that name which was given to me. He is a man who will adapt anything to his own immoral purpose and that, Gentlemen, is how you have fallen upon my magical name."

"What can you tell us about Mr Crowley?" asked Holmes quickly.

"Our paths have crossed on a number of occasions. Indeed, in the case that I know you were engaged to investigate, that of the continuing argument between MacGregor Mathers and the new leaders of the Golden Dawn, it was my duty on one night to have the police restrain Aleister Crowley from trespass on the holy site of our hidden church."

"Would it be, then, your idea that Aleister Crowley was somehow instrumental in the planting of these hearts and daggers?" asked Holmes.

"Indeed it would be, Mr Holmes. It has all the traits of a piece of his work – though I have heard reports that he is currently not in the country."

"Then, what is your view of the case as it stands?"

"I have no certain explanation, but you would be well advised to look at those people who are familiar with his work," replied Yeats in stern tone.

"Are you not, then, a perfect suspect? For you not only foresaw the discoveries of earlier today but must also be familiar with the work of Aleister Crowley."

"Indeed, it would look like that but I assure you that I would never sink to a practice that is similar in technique to that used by Aleister Crowley. I would never be involved in a diabolical use of instruments available to an adept."

"You mean by that, I presume, that you would not use a dagger or a heart for ritual purpose?"

"Exactly my point."

"Then, Mr Yeats, your own symbol is that of the rose."

"How on earth would you know such a thing?"

"There is no mystery I assure you. Whereas your lines of verse may have a seemingly innocent meaning to the likes of Mrs Hudson, I know that your real meaning is hidden behind your use of some beautiful words. It is not a difficult deduction to realise that the verse you quoted earlier is based on the magical world, in which you believe strongly. Further, I would suggest that your own personal symbol is that of the rose. The rose in your poetry accounts for your feeling which is strongly centred on your occult beliefs."

"It seems obvious when you explain it, and, indeed, you are correct: but you are one of a select few who has interpreted my work in this way."

Silence descended on the room with Yeats's closing remark. Sherlock Holmes leant back in his chair and relit the pipe he had deserted in his passion for the interview. The disconcerting quiet extended over a lengthy period in which I fully expected Yeats to leave our apartment but he remained in his chair, nervously grasping the fine teacup precariously between his delicate hands. Holmes looked up once or twice, seemingly to check that our visitor was still with us. Each of these glances was met with a short, nervous smile. On the final occasion of Holmes raising his eyes above the level of his pipe he commenced clarification of one of the points raised by the interview.

"I think I have a clear understanding of the case and although it must surely be one of the most disturbing, it will also prove to be quite unique. There is, however, one point on which you might shed light. You mention that the symbolism of the heart and dagger is part of a ritual but what can we expect to be at the core of the future – if it has not already happened – ceremony?"

"It is not easy to say, since rituals will vary in content dependent upon the required result. The hearts have been used as spiritual markers and are commonly known as talismans. I can only guess at the reason these talismans have been put in place."

"Then you can surely afford me a theory. It will be a waste of my time if the ritual turns out to be innocent within the eyes of the law. Indeed, if no crime has been or will be committed with respect to these gruesome discoveries there is little point in me continuing with this case. Perhaps you could tell me of the worst position?"

"Spiritually, the worst position is more grave than we as mortal men could ever attempt to comprehend, but as far as material crime is concerned I would suggest that the worst possibility would be nothing short of murder."

"Which may be linked to the disappearance of Anna Giles, no doubt."

"Who?" asked Yeats.

"A prostitute, reported missing."

"I had no idea," replied Yeats.

"Now, before I think through the courses of action available to us I should like to know why it is that you have such loathing of Aleister Crowley. The greater the knowledge we have of the man, the closer we step towards determining motive."

"It is simple, Mr Holmes. Aleister Crowley indulges in immoral sexual behaviour, which is too prevalent amongst men. He engages in perverse sexual practices, which I despise. We, in the Golden Dawn, are members of a mystical society, and a mystical society cannot be a moral reformatory."

"He sounds more and more like a suspect, but there must be something more to your dislike of him than your repugnance of his private life. After all, that is, presumably, little to do with his magical practices," replied Holmes dryly.

"You are entitled to your own opinion, Mr Holmes, and that opinion shall differ from mine for as long as I live, of that you can be sure."

"Then I think our business is concluded. If you have any further information, we would be grateful to hear it at the earliest opportunity."

"But you have not heard about the new vision I had last night, Mr Holmes!"

"What?" we both cried at once.

CHAPTER FOUR
The Third Heart

".......And that is all that I remember," was the end of Yeats's explanation of his vision. He had told us of another dream which he had about the time his first vision was 'manifested'. He spoke of the scenes in his dream which, down to the smallest detail, were the same as those that had come to him the previous night but for one fact – that the heart was buried in a different location. We had little difficulty in associating his first vision with the heart found in Mitre Square. Although Yeats claimed never to have been to Mitre Square himself, the description he gave was unnervingly accurate.

"There may be something to what you have told us thus far, Mr Yeats," conceded Holmes, "But if we are to take this further, we need to know exactly where we can find the new heart you have seen in your," Holmes paused, "'vision' – for that may be another clue as to the whereabouts of this prostitute. We need a complete description and the name of a place."

"Well, Mr Holmes, it is not easy. I have already told you all that I know, that I feel the place to be close to this Mitre Square you have told me about and also that the place is in the East End of London. I do have a name, but I can't say it is reliable."

"Come, man, let us have it," cried Holmes.

"There was a voice in my dream which spoke of two place names, two B's – I think the first was definitely Berner, and the second sounded like Butty."

"And you tell us that the heart is to be found in the rear yard of a house. Of that you are sure?"

"Indeed I am, Mr Holmes. I quite distinctly saw the heart lying behind some discarded timber in the back yard of a very modest dwelling. The housing itself was similar to those cramped dwellings found in the East End."

"Then we have something," said Holmes as he jumped from his seat to retrieve a number of loose sheets of paper. He laid them out on the table, whereupon I saw that they were maps of the East End. Holmes took his magnifying glass and bent over them. "Berner, Butty," he murmured under his breath as his finger traced through areas in order, starting from the Bishopsgate Ward, running through Portsoken Ward to Aldgate. Seeing that there was nothing in this vertical strip, he began again from the top with the Spitalfields ward, going south as far as the Royal Mint on the edge of the Wapping Ward. His breathing was heavy and his hand shook, but the further he went in his methodical search, the less optimistic we both became. It was on his fourth strip, however, when he gave a cry of delight. His finger rested in the Whitechapel area.

"What is it, Holmes?'

"It is too much to be coincidence, Watson, here we have a street called Berner

Street, and, running parallel to it, with a line of houses separating the two, is a street of the name Batty. Let us see if we can find this new 'heart'. Thank you, Mr Yeats."

"But how will we ever be able to find the exact point? The people of the area are not going to be sympathetic to a request to search their back yards, not to mention Lestrade's aversion to our activities."

"Ah," said Holmes, who was already in the process of putting his cloak on, "Is it not true to say, Mr Yeats, that, given your sensitivity to such things, you would be able to feel when the object was in close proximity?"

"I should think so, Mr Holmes, though you ask a lot. Any object, such as that which has been described to me, will be charged with a huge amount of magical energy. I am sure that I will be able to feel the energy and direct you, though it is a dangerous pursuit."

"Not so dangerous as murder, Mr Yeats."

Holmes walked out of the door and I was left to urge the nervous Yeats to hurry into his outdoor clothes to meet the cold that awaited us outside. The sun had already set, so I took the lamp we kept in the cupboard at the top of the stairs before joining Holmes in the street. Yeats caught us up just as a cab pulled in alongside us and a familiar figure jumped from it.

"Holmes, I hope you have not forgotten our appointment," said Lestrade shortly.

"Indeed not, Inspector, but there are more pressing matters for us to pursue. If I am not very much mistaken we are on the verge of another terrible discovery."

"Then I am duty bound to come with you, Holmes," replied Lestrade, whose eyes were glazed over with tiredness.

"We shall take your carriage and make haste to the spot we have marked to find our next instalment of treasure."

"Wait one moment, Holmes. Who the devil is this?" asked the Inspector, looking aghast at the emerging figure of Yeats who was having some difficulty with the buttons on his large coat.

"Ah, this is Mr Thompson," replied Holmes, without hesitation, "He has been a vital source of information and we are most grateful to him."

Yeats looked up at Holmes with a smile, as if acknowledging gratefully his help in maintaining anonymity.

"You had better explain on our way, Holmes. Where are we going?"

"The Commercial Road, on the East Side of Aldgate."

The piles of snow which had delayed our journey that morning had thawed somewhat during the day but the cold of the night was freezing over the roads. The cobbles had that dangerous sparkle to them that every cabman is wise to respect.

"So how did you come to acquire your information, Mr Thompson?' asked Inspector Lestrade as we headed our way down Oxford Street.

"Now, now Inspector, you have played my game before and should know that my methods are kept to myself until the time I decide to explain them," interjected Holmes, just as Yeats was beginning to ponder on his reply. The nervous jump from our 'informant' had not gone unnoticed by Lestrade, however, and I felt sure that unless we could clear the ugly business up quickly, eyes would once again fall on Yeats as a prime suspect. "But do tell me how you got on with the search of the other sites of Jack the Ripper murders?"

"It will come, Mr Holmes, you mark my words. Jack the Ripper is back and will not escape us for a second time. He is handing us clues, similar to those he had posted the first time around – when we find Anna Giles, you will regret mocking me."

"Then you found some evidence at the other Ripper murder sites?"

"Not as such, Mr Holmes, there was nothing. But I am confident that he will not leave them unattended. It is a trait in the mind of the criminal to return to the place he has previously committed a crime. I have put men discreetly in position to watch over the three places, all hours of the day."

The thought of some of Lestrade's men acting discreetly brought a smile to Holmes's face. "You are wasting your time, Lestrade, you can be assured of that. The man we are looking for is using the legend of Jack the Ripper as a screen to hide his true activities."

"And how can you be so sure of that, Holmes? It was you yourself who pointed out that the man we are looking for is left-handed. If you would care to look over our notes of the Ripper case, you will also notice that the Ripper himself was left handed. You cannot make me believe that is mere coincidence."

"I am not trying to make you believe anything, Inspector, you have your theories and I have mine. But one in ten of our fellow countrymen are left handed and I do not see that a one in ten chance cannot be coincidental. If you are a betting man Inspector, you should surely favour such odds if they were given."

"Then, what is your theory, Holmes?' asked the disgruntled policeman.

"In good time, Inspector, in good time. It is more important that we track down the man responsible for this dastardly act."

"But, surely we are looking for Jack the Ripper? I do not understand how you can dismiss this theory out of hand. What do you know of the Ripper case? You speak as if he was dead."

"Probably is," replied Holmes mysteriously.

This was as far as the conversation went since Holmes interrupted it to urge the driver on, not an action likely to endear him any further to the Inspector. Yeats was sitting next to me, moving about on his seat nervously. His expression of mild goodwill had changed dramatically on the realisation that he was now involved with the police themselves and, although Holmes had afforded him some protection, I knew that he was not altogether sure of Holmes's word. Meanwhile, as we plunged on through the city, it grew colder. The streets were dark and deserted, except for a few foolhardy travellers. We turned eventually onto the Commercial Road, a point at which most cabs refuse to cross.

Holmes, who had been lost in thought throughout the journey through the city, now turned his attention to the side of the streets that were speeding past our windows. On our left were a few large warehouses, behind which were squeezed the squalid lines of houses that were the disgraceful refuges of the poverty that plagues our great city. Yet the backbone of our city was to be found amongst the inhabitants of this district, the men on whose labour we rely upon. Many ranks of infantry men had been recruited from these very streets in order that they may carry the nation's flag into the battles in Afghanistan and Africa. To the south were the docks where the labouring classes huddled. As we travelled further along Commercial Street, shadows of men and women ducked from our vision under the dimly lit arches of the alleyways, a thousand and more spirits attending to their business, honest or dishonest.

We pulled up to a slower pace as we passed the cooperage, after which there was a stable where the driver had planned to leave the carriage, under the watchful eye of the grooms who would see that no harm came to it. The snow lay thickly on the ground, unlike in the city, and it crunched crisply under our feet as we made our way a few yards eastwards. We turned into Berner Street and were immediately plunged into almost complete darkness, though there was the briefest glimpses of fires crackling in nearby windows when our eyes had accustomed themselves. Holmes held a hand up to halt us in the middle of the road.

"I hope you are sure about this, Holmes," said Lestrade suddenly. He had not uttered a word from the cab once we had crossed the threshold into the Whitechapel area and he was now showing signs of acute nerves.

"I am sure of it, Lestrade. Besides, we must make our work as hastily as possible before the locals decide they do not care for the look of us or our ways," replied Holmes, taking a long sideways glance at the policeman who, although not in uniform, might be identified as an unwelcome presence by the local inhabitants.

Holmes took a lamp from Lestrade and waited while I lit mine. Once we had enough illumination to make our way down the darkened street, we set off. Yeats remained silent and I could see from his expression that he had as many misgivings as the Inspector about the area in to which we had plunged.

"Mr Thompson, perhaps you would be good enough to guide us to the spot you were telling me about." Holmes handed Yeats the lamp so that he may guide himself.

"Yes, and as quick as you like," said Lestrade from behind.

We walked on in silence, listening for the crunch of other footsteps in the snow from the small darkened side streets which were designed seemingly for the purpose of those leaving their 'business' until nightfall. But we had not walked more than fifty yards when a voice rang out into the still night and seemed to hang in the blackness. It was only Holmes who did not jump. It said:

"Come on, what's the game here, I've told you before to keep well away from my yard, else you will be receiving the strong end of my whip."

"It is alright, Sir, we mean you no harm," returned Holmes, in a calming tone. His voice was steady and as strong as would be expected from someone born into this neighbourhood.

"Why, I do believe it to be Mr Holmes. How are you, Sir?' The voice was softer on realising that we did not present the threat first feared and the body of the man seemed to appear from nowhere in front of us. The bulky man had removed his cap and held it in front of him, whilst the other hand carried one of the largest whips I had ever seen. His huge head was bald apart from a few black wisps of hair around the sides. As he spoke, shadows obscured him from close examination but it was obvious from his red complexion that he had been working hard in the stable from which he had emerged. The stables were only dimly visible, but the smell was unmistakable.

"Ah, Mr Dunstan, I had forgotten that this was your neighbourhood," said Holmes, "But please replace your cap, the night is bitter cold and not a time to stand on ceremony."

"Thank you, Mr Holmes, may I be so bold as to enquire what brings you into this area at such a dangerous time of night. There have been disturbances since the weather has set in bad. Some of the docks have been closed because of the ice and there is no work."

"We may well need your assistance, Mr Dunstan, and it is a most generous offer," replied Holmes amiably, before turning to us, "This is Mr Dunstan, he owns this fine set of stables. I had the pleasure of working on a most intriguing case some years ago when a number of his animals were suddenly struck lame."

"And most successful you were too, Mr Holmes, there is surely no better brain in the country. Any assistance I can give will be all my pleasure."

"Well," said Holmes, "Maybe Mr Thompson has something for us here?"

I had completely forgotten about Yeats who had been hunched up next to me during the conversation, as had Inspector Lestrade – whose mind was presumably puzzling over the crimes which had affected this amenable stable owner. Yeats was shivering, though not, I guessed, from the cold.

"It is close, Mr Holmes, of that I am sure, and it is to our left," was all Yeats said in reply.

Holmes took his cue and stalked purposefully to the side of the road, whereupon the gates of Mr Dunstan's stables suddenly appeared to us. Yeats drew up alongside me and then headed straight into the yard. Once past the gates, the sides of the yard could be seen as lamps hung from the stable buildings and were valiant in their attempt to cut light through the darkest of nights. Yeats led us to the centre of the cobbled area and looked around him. Lining all sides of the yard were closed stable doors from which, occasionally, the sound of a horse could be heard.

"Which direction do we want?" asked Holmes impatiently.

"Here, what is this?" enquired Lestrade, who was looking more at ease once the gates to the yard had been closed behind us. "Is this Mr Thompson a blood hound?"

"I have asked you not to question my methods, Inspector. The less interruption Mr Thompson has, the quicker we can be away from this area. Surely you would be agreeable to that reasoning?"

Lestrade didn't reply, and, on turning, he suddenly said, "Where is he going now?"

All of us turned to see the figure of Yeats moving stealthily away from us, heading due south to one of the ranks of stable buildings. He walked on, trance-like, seemingly unaware of what was being said about him by the Inspector. Holmes was the first to react and, with a few quick bounds, was alongside Yeats.

"Can you tell me where it is, Thompson?' he demanded.

"I am very close, Mr Holmes, but I do not think it is in this stable, it is just the other side," replied Yeats. By this time, we had run up against one of the stables and Holmes had already made to unlock it.

"Are you sure it cannot be in the stable?" asked Holmes.

"If it were in the stable, that horse would not be so quiet, that I can guarantee. No, it is definitely past the stable."

Holmes turned back to Dunstan who was looking confused under the faint light of the gas lamps. "It appears that we have wasted our time in your stables, Mr Dunstan, and that the object we search for must be in the first of those houses that lie behind this stable row."

"But that is my own house, Mr Holmes. What is it that you are searching for?"

"Trust me – all will be revealed, and all too graphically if we are correct in our supposition. Time is of the essence, Mr Dunstan, so maybe you could guide us to your back yard."

"Of course, Mr Holmes, anything to oblige you, Sir. There is a gate in the cor-ner of this yard that will take us straight through, follow me and I will show you."

Dunstan lead the way towards the corner of the stable yard, towards an area of pitch blackness. Once in the corner of the compound, our guide lifted the latch on a gate and led us through to the small back yard of the end terrace house that fronted onto Berner Street.

As soon as we were in Mr Dunstan's back yard, Yeats suddenly cried, "It is here, it is there. Quick look down, I can feel it, oh how horrible it must be!" He was shaking, but held a hand out and with that he was pointing at a patch of earth that had supported numerous plants until the cold weather had killed them off.

"Then we must dig," said Holmes quickly, "Have you a shovel handy, Mr Dunstan?'

Mr Dunstan did not reply, but retraced his steps quickly back towards the stable yard. He returned with two shovels, one of which he handed to Holmes and the other I snatched from him.

"Dig, Watson, dig!" cried Holmes as the blade of his shovel sank into the ground. I did as requested and joined him in his frantic efforts to unearth the hidden clue.

It was not long to wait, for no sooner had we sifted through three shovelfuls of earth, did my hand fall on a hard, irregular object. I held it aloft and Holmes picked the lamp from the ground to see what we had found. In that dark atmosphere, the object was of the most hideous nature one could ever imagine. We recognised our find straight away – a heart, with a small dagger plunged deep into its middle.

Our attention was taken, however, by the bloodcurdling scream that sounded directly behind us. We turned just in time to see Yeats fall heavily into unconsciousness on the hard cold floor. As I bent down to help him, I saw his features contorted into a look of absolute fear.

* * *

I was not the only person who spent the whole night awake, for Sherlock Holmes worked enthusiastically through the papers he had written on our current case. Even if I had been able to sleep after our recent adventure in Whitechapel, I should still have needed to stay awake in order that I could attend to our patient who had lapsed into a serious fever. With the help of Lestrade and the unnerved Mr Dunstan, we had managed to carry Yeats to the carriage and from there we drove to Baker Street, where he was deposited on my bed and where he has remained ever since, occasionally regaining consciousness and shouting madly, but in the main lying absolutely still. The expression on his face was a contorted picture of living fear.

I took a break from tending him for a few minutes so that I could warm myself by the fire and have a full pipe without fear of the smoke irritating the gravely ill man. As I looked out of the window, I could see that the snow had once again begun to fall and was reflecting off the rising sun as it passed the window on its way to the drifts that were once again piling themselves against the sides of Baker Street. I was restless though and, rather than sit by myself, wandered around the room, picking books that looked of interest from the numerous shelves and replacing them once I had given the room a full circuit.

"Watson, that is a most infuriating habit you have of being quite restless while I am trying to concentrate," piped up Holmes from the table. Although he spoke in harsh tones directed straight at me, he did not look up from the page he was studying.

"Well, have we any theories to be going on with?" I asked, wanting some conversation to break the boredom of tending a patient whose best cure lay in the hands of nature.

"They are not coming to mind at present, Watson, no hypothesis fits all facts fully. It really is one of the queerest cases I have ever had the pleasure to decipher. I believe the answer lies in activities we, ourselves, have little knowledge of. It is difficult working with a mind that is set on believing in the world of the 'supernatural', for that is apparently the way our suspect is being motivated in his actions. But I cannot help thinking that the solution is right in front of my eyes. If I did not know better, I would be inclined to agree with Lestrade in his theory that Jack the Ripper is once again prowling the streets. Tell me, how is the patient? I have some questions I need him to answer."

"You may not get the chance, Holmes, he is in a very deep fevered sleep."

"Then what is your diagnosis, Watson?'

"I am at a loss to explain it, Holmes. Whilst obviously in a state of shock – he also exhibits signs of a tropical fever, including delirium. When semiconscious, the delirium sets in, yet when he regains consciousness, which has happened from time to time, he seems to be of sound mind for a moment before lapsing back under. I know of nothing quite like it, I shall need to call in a specialist for advice. Indeed, my first stop will be Professor Whilley, the foremost expert on nervous disorders." In spite of the opportunity to talk about Yeats's condition, I was more restless than before. There is nothing worse for a doctor than the inability to help a patient.

"I should be grateful for some tea if it is not too much to ask," came a voice from the bedroom. I whirled round to see Yeats making his way towards the fire. In that briefest of moments, I saw that he was exhausted but also sheepish.

"My Dear Fellow, you should not raise yourself from that bed," I heard myself saying, "You have been delirious and the best thing is complete rest until that time when we can understand more fully what ails you so."

"You need not worry, Dr Watson, I understand fully my symptoms and can say that the worst has passed."

"By all the…. How can you have any knowledge of your symptoms? You have not even been conscious."

"Fever, delirium, in and out of consciousness and occasionally seeming of sound mind. It has happened before, and I dare say it will happen again," replied Yeats with a slight smile.

I was astonished, scarcely believing my eyes. It was Holmes who moved first, he paced over to the fireplace and led Yeats into a chair. I studied his face and his movements, sure that he was in some way manoeuvring himself in unconsciousness, much the same way as people do when sleep walking, but found that his face was regaining its natural colour and that his movement of limbs was completely free from nervous tension.

"Come now, Watson, our friend here has come through a terrible ordeal, he needs some tea – you yourself heard him say so," said Holmes, which stirred me out of my inaction. I called Mrs Hudson who came to us in longer than five minutes I fancy and, when she did, she was wrapped in a huge dressing gown. "We shall need some tea, Mrs Hudson," said Holmes in a sweet voice, "And I apologise for bringing you from your bed at such an early hour."

"That is quite alright, it shan't be a moment," she replied, having kept her eye fixed on Yeats.

"Now, Yeats," said Holmes in a crisp voice, "You said that you have experienced this before and that you know what your medical complaint is?"

"Yes, though I would not strictly class it as a medical complaint for in its own way it is a matter for a psychologist. The fact of the matter is that, if you are like me and are sensitive to magical studies, you will feel energy from magical artefacts. You will remember that I led you to the heart last night, only being able to do so because I was sensitive to the energy it was emitting. This energy was very strong, which basically means that the man who made the artefact, who drove the dagger through the heart, is a magician of considerable power. On coming into contact with the heart, it had a seemingly magical but, alas, adverse effect on my mind."

"I do not quite follow why it should have such an effect on you as an individual. Why should it be an adverse effect?" I asked, unsure of the answer Yeats had given.

"The three hearts and daggers you have uncovered are obviously part of a much larger ritual. They are used as protection for the larger activity. Consequently, these talismans are used to warn people away from the site of the main ritual. It is a common enough phenomenon but I have never known a ring of magical protection to be so powerful ...."

"That is it!" cried Holmes suddenly, stopping Yeats in mid flow and rushing towards the table. He grabbed a large sheet of paper and returned to spread it on the floor between us. "Tell me what you mean by a ring of protection."

"Basically just that; a magician will surround himself by a ring of talismans, to ward off any interruption. This ring is also used as a way of concentrating all the magical energy available."

"Then we have made progress at last. But, before I explain, please tell me whether I am correct in recalling the pentagram to be a powerful symbol to people indulging in occult activity?" urged Holmes.

"That is correct, it is deemed to be a very powerful symbol indeed. Though I must say that I myself do not use it," replied Yeats.

"Ah, but you do, Mr Yeats. Surely the symbol of the rose is merely an extension of the pentagram. The rose is depicted as having five petals. Now, if you took each petal as representing a point and that the petals were evenly spaced, then would it not be that the rose does represent a more picturesque pentagram?"

"Why, Mr Holmes, I do believe you are right," said Yeats, grinning slyly.

"I do not see what this has to do with our case, Holmes, surely you do not still think Mr Yeats here to be involved?"

"Far from it, Watson. On the contrary, Mr Yeats has helped, yet again. But look here." Holmes leant over the spread of paper he had lain on the floor and was pointing to three marks he had made. "This is a map of the area we are dealing with and I have marked on the exact points where hearts with daggers have been found. Now, my theory is that the places where the hearts were left are an integral part of the ritual as a whole. The first two, those found in Mitre Square and Dorset Street are two points in a pentagram and are adjacent to each other. But it does not follow that the stable yard in Berner Street is another adjacent point, so it must therefore be the single point in the pentagram that is not adjacent to either of the others."

It was at this stage that Holmes took a pencil and began to draw lines between all the three points he had marked. He then set to working out where the missing two points were. Within a couple of minutes, he had drawn a thick black outline, representing the pentagram and including two points that had not yet been discussed.

"Yes, I think we have it. From this map, I would predict that we would find a heart and dagger at each of these two further points. The first one is close to the Roman Catholic Boy's School in Hamber Street, just north of the Fenchurch Street rail line. The second is a long way to the north, almost due east of Dorset Street. We should find our heart and dagger somewhere in this block of houses between Casson Street and Great Garden Street."

"Why, that is brilliant, Holmes."

"Not at all, Watson, a mere application of logic. Though it does not get us too far, for, if I am correct, we shall just end up with two more of these wretched objects."

I looked across at Yeats. He wanted to say something, but his state of high nerves had descended once more upon him.

"You need not worry, Mr Yeats," said Holmes, "We shall not need your assistance for this, rest assured. I shall send message to Lestrade, requiring him to give a thorough search of the areas, which shall leave us free for the rest of the day to make other avenues of enquiry. Wait a moment – Mr Yeats – what was it you said about a ring of protection? Surely if the person is to be believed in forming this ring of protection, they would have taken the ritual at its centre? And, as for the ritual, there is the coincidence of the missing prostitute – Anna Giles. Would she be involved in this ritual, I wonder?"

"Yes, it is possible," replied Yeats gloomily.

"Then I just have to find the centre of this pentagram and we have a mark of the place where the crime has or, at least, will take place." Holmes began taking further measurements across the map and making marks here and there. When he finally drew a circle around the centre point, he looked up, the excitement having gone from his expression. "This is no good. Look where the centre falls; right in the centre of the junction between Whitechapel High Street and Commercial Road. In fact, right in the middle of one of those tram junctions. Surely, if the ritual took place here, we would have heard about it by now, I could not think of a busier junction in the whole of the East End."

"Yes, Holmes," I replied, "But as you yourself have said, it may not have happened yet."

"Then that is our only course of action, Watson. I must whip up the Baker Street Irregulars and place them firmly on duty at that point, sending reports to me of anything out of the ordinary. Meanwhile, I think our day will not be wasted if we have a closer look at these daggers."

Holmes left us for almost an hour on, what I presumed to be, a trip to round up his faithful army of street urchins and send them forward on their task. He returned with renewed vigour and promptly asked Mr Yeats, who had fallen asleep in his chair, if he would mind helping for a while longer.

"I should feel much obliged if you were to give me an opinion on the daggers we have found. I have two in my possession at this very moment."

"But, Holmes," I protested, I would urge you to desist from this course of action, it could have a most adverse effect on our guest if he were to be placed in contact with those accursed objects again."

"It is alright, Dr Watson," replied Yeats, "So long as the dagger is pulled from the heart, the magical energy is gone and I shall be in no danger."

"Good, then I should like you to examine this carefully," said Holmes, handing him one of the daggers he had concealed in his pocket, "Tell me all you know about it."

"Well," replied Yeats, after turning it over under his eye for some moments, "It is definitely a ritual dagger, French in origin for it has a most distinct design, and this skull carving is commonly found amongst the Monks of central France. But it has been adapted for a very individual purpose, as all these markings on the handle have been added after the original manufacture."

"I had noticed as much from the relative softness of the wood exposed by the carvings," replied Holmes.

"Yes, but also these symbols are relatively new and would not have been used at the time the daggers were originally made. They are, to my mind, linked to the teachings of those who follow in the worship of the Goddess Hekate. It is unusual for any traditional occultist to have anything to do with the resurgence of interest in this Goddess of the Underworld."

"Where would you obtain such a set of items?" asked Holmes suddenly.

"Your guess is as good as mine, Mr Holmes. The daggers are old – so perhaps they might be found in an antique shop. If my memory serves me correctly, they would originally have been limited to making only three sets of each particular design and each set would have consisted of six daggers in total."

"Three sixes?" asked Holmes.

"The number of the Devil," replied Yeats.

"But I thought you said they were manufactured by monks?' I asked quickly.

"Yes indeed, Dr Watson, though I do not think they were always used as Christian symbols."

"This is very interesting, Mr Yeats," said Holmes, "And at the same time most disturbing. If our theory is correct, and Lestrade manages to find the two other daggers at the points in East London we have deduced, then that only accounts for five of the daggers."

"It might help you to know that traditionally there would be five daggers of this size, accompanied by one of greater length, which would be used as the tool for sacrifice," said Yeats.

"Sacrifice? Then this is indeed grave. We must waste no little time in our search for the shop that has sold these daggers. I shall need to find an old acquaintance of mine, for he may save us some effort, but a full day lies ahead of us if we are to prevent what is looking more and more to be a crime in the form of an occult sacrifice."

CHAPTER SIX
The Return Of The Scarlet Woman

It may have been presumption on my own part, but when Sherlock Holmes had asked me to accompany him on his visit to his antiques expert that afternoon, I was surprised to find that, instead of heading into the antique shops of the West End, we travelled much on the same route as we had the previous night. The driver of the hansom cab had refused to take us any further than the Tower for fear, he said, of the unrest in the East End. We alighted close to the Royal Mint, whereupon Holmes began to lead us through small alleys and back streets, until we eventually emerged on the south side of the Commercial Road. In the light of day, the area we had visited the night before certainly did not have the same sense of serious foreboding. Milder weather had set in and people were walking along the pavements about their everyday business. The snow was beginning to melt and slush was running through the gutters, lapping up at our feet as we made our way across the road.

Holmes pulled a woman to one side as she attempted to bustle past us and muttered a few words. She gave him a reply before setting off again, with her head down against the wind that was trapped along the street. "Well, Watson, our transport should be with us very shortly," said Holmes.

No sooner had I thought about asking him where we were going, did the tram come along the street and stop for us to get on. In all probability, it was only the second or third time I had travelled in this new way, but Holmes bounded up into the carriage as if it was his normal mode of transport. The conductor was arguing with one of the passengers about a fare for poultry, which almost came to blows, but, once a burly labourer had stepped in and told them he would be late for work if they did not get a move on, the conductor signalled and we were on our way.

The East End of London, as I have often remarked, is unique. Within its ranks it holds some of the meanest criminals, yet it has spirit that, I fancy, could not be readily broken under any condition. I looked out of the window, caught in the fascinating surroundings through which we were travelling. There was no end to the different types of people. There were Chinamen, sailors, labourers, tramps, soldiers on leave, dock workers. Only one thing was the common link between them all; poverty – a poverty that shames our country.

The tram stopped next to the lock that led to the Regents Dock, whereupon both the dock worker and the man with his two chickens got off and disappeared in different directions. The tram moved forward again and we were engulfed in hordes of sailors making their way across the road – a large ship having come into dock, ensuring that the local public houses were soon to be filled.

We probably only went another half a mile before Holmes tapped me on the shoulder and made his way to the rear of the tram. We alighted and found ourselves on the interchange with the East India Dock road. Without hesitating, Holmes led us up a main road in the direction of the Limehouse Cut, but stopped short and disappeared into a public house that I had not even noticed. I followed him through the clouds of tobacco smoke that had risen from the bar below. The density of the smoke increased considerably as we walked down the wooden staircase and into the crowded room. Sailors were already sitting around numerous small tables and were conversing loudly with each other in a foreign tongue – which I took to be Dutch. Holmes was impervious to the curious and hostile stares as he made his way towards the bar.

"Watson, I shall take a beer, could I get you one of the same?" he asked once he had caught the landlord's attention and had turned to me.

"Certainly, Holmes," I replied, but no sooner had I looked for some reaction to our presence from the men pushing against us, did a rather large man push his way through and stand in front of me.

"Did you just say 'Holmes?'" he ordered, looking down at me through over-hanging eyebrows that matched in colour and thickness his large black beard. I felt my stomach turn over, thinking we had encountered a previous adversary of Holmes's.

"Why, if it is not Foreman Nailer?' said Holmes, turning around with our drinks. The whole of the room had fallen deadly quiet and all eyes were firmly fixed on the pair. Those men nearest to us, shuffled backwards, away from trouble. The large man glared down at Holmes, who returned a stony stare for some moments before saying, "Would you care to drink with me?"

"I should be the one to buy you a drink, my friend," came the reply, to the astonishment of all, "I shall get yourself and your friend here the next one." Then, in the next breath he turned to the other drinkers and shouted, "Well, what are you lot staring at? Mind your own business!"

"Mr Nailer, this here is my friend and colleague, Dr Watson," said Holmes as he handed me my glass of beer.

"Any friend of yours is welcome here, Mr Holmes," replied the man in his strong voice. "But what brings you to our thieves' den?"

"I need some information from you, assuming that is, you are still working on the docks?" said Holmes.

"That I am, Mr Holmes. Perhaps it is best if we leave this rabble for somewhere quieter." Nailer picked up an ornate and expensive tankard, full to the brim with ale, and led us to the end of the bar and into a room in the back where there was a dying fire and four worn chairs. There was also an old wooden table which could have served as a card-table for the landlord and his cronies.

"Anything you want to know, Mr Holmes, just ask me. I am always in your debt."

"Most of the ships from the continent pass into your docks, do they not?" replied Holmes to Nailer's offer.

"That they do, Mr Holmes, and I could tell you all you want to know of those that go elsewhere."

"Good, then I need to know about a small cargo that would probably have made its way from France." Holmes took one of the small daggers from his pocket and handed it to our informant. "There are probably three sets of these, coming from the south of France, though I do not know when they would have arrived."

The man took the dagger and looked it over, his face the picture of concentration. "Someone has tampered with it?" he said suddenly, his face brightening as if he recognised it.

"Most probably, the carvings in the handle have been added, I should think after it came in through the docks. I am sure that you will agree when I say it is a somewhat unusual cargo and would have been brought to your attention."

"They certainly were, but we had no use for them, they seemed fairly worthless."

"What is this?" I cried, unable to help myself, "You quite readily admit to stealing cargo?"

"That is not of importance, Watson," came the sharp rebuke from Holmes.

"We see it as a tax, Dr Watson, similar to all those duties paid in ports across the world." Nailer had a smile on his face, that of a powerful man with all the respect necessary to make his position impregnable, before returning his attention to Holmes, "I know that these knives arrived from Marseilles, not more than a month since."

"Then you could find out where they went?" said Holmes quickly, the excitement showing in his smile.

"Not a problem, Mr Holmes. It would not take me more than twenty minutes to look up the record. If you should care to wait here, I shall return with all you need to know."

"That would be splendid," replied Holmes, "Though you could perhaps get us that beer you offered earlier."

The large man left the room, buttoning up his coat as he did so, and we were left alone to await his return. No sooner had Holmes removed a cigarette from his case then the landlord entered the room and silently placed two glasses of beer on the table. He left without saying a word and Holmes did not even acknowledge the interruption.

I fancy it was slightly more than the promised twenty minutes before Nailer returned. "You bring us good news, I see," said Holmes.

"Indeed, I do, Mr Holmes, and I am only too pleased to be of service. Here is the address of the shop that the cargo was bound for, though I do not know it myself," he replied, handing Holmes a scrap of paper.

"Ah, it is well away from your area," said Holmes, with a good humoured grin. "I know that is a very rare occasion when you travel further north than Stepney."

"You know me too well, Mr Holmes. The ship came in three weeks ago and returned the day after. It was a French crew, I could find out the name of the captain if you like?"

"That will not be necessary, Nailer, all the information we require is on this piece of paper. Thank you very much for your help. Come along, Watson, if we are quick, we may be able to make the journey before the shop closes."

It was not necessary to take the tram away from the heart of the docks, for Nailer had persuaded a cabman who had been drinking in a dark corner, to get his horse ready and take us wherever we wished. As it turned out, Holmes ordered him to take us to Islington since, I found out during the journey, this was where we were to find the shop where the three sets of daggers had been taken. The sun had already set by the time we were travelling along Upper Street and Holmes was looking with some dismay at the large number of shops that were locking up for the day. He urged the cab driver on with all haste, which was not taken in all grace, our man not being in the best of spirits, having been taken away from his drink. Upper Street was poorly lit, only one in three lamps were shining when we turned into Essex Road. Holmes ordered the carriage to be stopped alongside a row of three antique shops, whereupon, on trying to pay the driver, was refused, brusquely – "The fare has already been taken care of."

The shop we wanted was already closed. Nevertheless, Holmes tapped loudly on the door with his stick. A light came on, towards the back of the shop and a shadow appeared. "We are closed, please call again tomorrow. We shall open at nine o'clock," came the frail voice of an old man.

"I am very sorry to bother you, Sir," replied Holmes in a strong, loud voice, "It is of utmost importance that we speak to you now."

"What is it you are after?" came the wary reply, "If it is about the desk, it has been sold already."

"No, it is not the desk. We would like to know whether you have some ceremonial knives we have been seeking for some time. They have originated in a monastery in France."

The catch on the door was lifted on hearing Holmes's question and a small opening let out a crack of light. "Those knives are not worth their bother, of that I am sure," replied the voice from inside. "I really would prefer it if you could come back tomorrow, my supper is ready."

"This will not take more than a couple of minutes, Sir," replied Holmes calmly.

The door opened up fully, though somewhat reluctantly, and we stepped into the shop. Immediately, I could feel the warmth of the fire that must have been burning in a back room and the heat seemed to increase the musty smell of the place. Looking around the small shop front, we were confronted with a mixture of seemingly expensive antiques. Holmes nudged me after a few moments and I followed the direction of his gaze to see that he had spotted a small oak case with its lid open. Inside nestled a set of six knives, five of which were exact replicas of the ones we had found sunk into real hearts. The sixth knife was possibly as much as three times the length of the others and its blade was considerably wider. On top of this knife, instead of the skull carving, there was a pentagram.

"Ah, just what we are searching for," said Holmes as he pushed past the shop owner and toward the set of knives.

"Yes, they are magnificent specimens, are they not? Certainly most collectable items," replied the small man who had placed a pair of spectacles on his nose and was hovering around the side of Holmes. "There are only three sets of these in existence, which should make them even more attractive to yourself."

"Well, that is indeed so, though I should like to know where the other sets are of course. I cannot make the purchase unless I am sure I can get my hands on all the other sets."

"Ah, I see," replied the man, his face dropping the sign of optimism that had briefly been evident. I can certainly let you have two of the sets, though I have sold the other, not more than one week since."

Holmes spun around on the man, sending him back a pace in nervousness. "It is essential that I have all three sets, else they are of little value to me. Perhaps you have some note of who the purchaser of the first set was? If I can ensure getting hold of that set, I should certainly make it worth your while to supply me with the other two sets."

"I shall see what I can do," replied the man, "If you could bear with me as I check my records."

Holmes followed the man to the back of the shop, where he took a book of ledgers and opened it out on a small table. "I am afraid that the young lady did not leave an address, if I recall she explained that she was leaving the country shortly."

"A young lady?" cried Holmes, "Perhaps you could give me a description?"

"Here, what is this?" replied the man, looking upon us with suspicion in his eyes.

"I admit that we are not looking to purchase these knives, and I should like to introduce myself as Sherlock Holmes, this is my companion, Dr Watson."

"The Sherlock Holmes? Well I never – You are taller than I had imagined."

"That idea is probably due, in part, to Dr Watson's somewhat inaccurate chronicles," replied Holmes sternly, "But it is of the utmost importance that we have a description of the woman in question."

"Well, my memory does not serve me very well and I cannot remember her giving me a name, but rarely have I seen such a picture of beauty. She was tall, all dressed in black, with deep dark eyes."

"Tell me about her voice, her demeanour and the reason she gave to purchasing this extraordinary set of knives."

"She gave little reason for why she wanted the knives, merely that she was conducting a study into the ancient rites of an obscure group of monks, ones that I have never heard of. Now that she has been brought to my attention in such a way however, I would try to explain her whole presence as somewhat mysterious. There was something deeply unsettling, something I find very hard to explain fully, though I hope you get my meaning?"

"I see," said Holmes, noncommittally, "Please try to describe her voice."

"Ah, now that is an easier question. It was surely from the mills of Lancashire, I could not mistake it, however subtle, for that is where my father came from, before he bought this shop and brought the family down with him."

"Then, Watson, we have the person we are looking for," said Holmes suddenly, "Our Scarlet Woman has returned once again. Tanith Hekaltey."

CHAPTER SEVEN
A Brutal Theory

We were met at Baker Street by quite a furore. In our apartment there were at least five people, arguing amongst themselves, and in the middle of them was our housekeeper, Mrs Hudson. As soon as she saw that we were in the doorway, she ran to Sherlock Holmes who, though not showing it, I am sure was as shocked as me at the scene in front of us.

"Oh, Mr Holmes, I have been trying to tell these gentlemen that it is not proper to descend on someone else's property and place bits of flesh on the table, no matter if they are the police," she said hurriedly.

"It is quite alright, Mrs Hudson, but please tell me where Mr Yeats has gone," replied Holmes.

"He went this afternoon, not long after you left. He said that if you want to contact him, he will be staying in Bedford Place."

"Thank you, Mrs Hudson, that will be all, apart from maybe cups of your splendid tea for all," said Holmes and turned to the small group of men, "Ah, Lestrade, have you some results for me? And you, Perkins, what do you bring me?"

As Lestrade stepped out of the way and the other police officers stepped back, two things were revealed. The first was the presence of the leader of the Baker Street Irregulars, but perhaps most surprising, were the two objects on the table. As with the three that had already been discovered, Lestrade had brought with him the final two hearts, complete with daggers lying by their side.

"Holmes, I took the liberty to remove the daggers from the hearts, in case your Mr Thompson was present again. But, as you can well see, after a thorough search of the areas you brought to our attention, we have discovered yet more of these abominable items. Now perhaps, you might be able to explain how you came to know of the whereabouts of these things and give me some explanation of just who this mysterious Mr Thompson is? For a start, the good Mrs Hudson has informed me his real name is a Mr Yeats. I am becoming rather tired of your wilful attempts to mislead me."

"I shall explain in good time, Inspector, but first I should like to hear if Perkins has any news of any developments in Whitechapel."

Holmes turned his attention to the young lad who was in turn looked at with some disdain by the two policemen who flanked him on either side. "We have no sighting, Mr Holmes, and that's a fact. The lads have kept sentry all day but, apart from a bar room brawl tumbling onto the street, there has been nothing."

At this, the room was plunged into silence. It appeared that only Lestrade had a slight grin spread across his face. Perkins dutifully tipped his cap to Holmes, ignored the policemen and left the room to carry on his mission.

"Now, Holmes, I demand an explanation," began Lestrade when Mrs Hudson had delivered the tea and returned downstairs. It seems obvious to me that you are on the wrong track, or perhaps you have been involved in this incident right from the start."

"Is that an accusation, Inspector?" said Holmes calmly.

"An observation, Mr Holmes. I should like to know how you have come by your discoveries thus far, why you still employ young ruffians to act as spies on the public and why you cannot accept the fact that Jack the Ripper has once again descended upon us – this prostitute, Anna Giles, has not returned. And, while you are at it, you may as well tell me where this Mr Yeats fits in, for never have I known such a suspicious character."

"So you still think you are chasing Jack the Ripper, Inspector? Surely I should have convinced you by showing you where these new hearts have been found, after all they have nothing to do with Jack the Ripper, do they?"

"The first two were too much of a coincidence, Holmes, of that I am sure. The fact that the discovery of the last three did not seem to fit, makes it all the more suspicious. Mark my words, Mr Holmes, I have noticed the part you have played in this investigation and I have a good mind to report you as obstructing an officer of the law. And as for this Mr Yeats, I should like you to give me the place of his residence so I may have an opportunity to question him. If you should like to talk about coincidence, I should very much like to point out that unique episode last night when an acquaintance of yours led us single-handed to a scene of a crime. He may know more about this missing prostitute than he is letting on."

"It does seem too much of a coincidence that our Mr Yeats knew where the third heart was and, in a curious way, he is an absolutely integral part of this queer case. Though I must warn you that it was I who deduced where we could find the final two artefacts."

"Artefacts?" cried Lestrade, "You make it sound as if we are dealing with a museum rather than a cold-blooded killer."

"Hot blooded, very hot blooded."

"I beg your pardon?"

"The perpetrator of these deeds. She is very hot blooded and that is the primary reason in her motives."

"There is something that you are keeping from me?"

"I should be grateful if I could retell my part of the investigation thus far, from the beginning, without further interruptions," replied Holmes.

The Inspector motioned for Holmes to begin the explanation, and did not say a word until Holmes had finished. Even at the point Holmes named Tanith Hekaltey, the Inspector merely raised his brows slightly. "So there we have it, Lestrade, quite a unique little case really, wouldn't you say?"

"But this Mr Yeats, if it is as you say, Holmes, then surely he must be involved. Here, you and Dr Watson have not been taken in by this occult nonsense, you do not believe his story, or his feigning of ill health?"

"I can vouch that he was in a very serious condition and that he could not have put it on," I suddenly said.

"And, no matter what his true knowledge of the matter is, I can vouch that he is certainly not involved – he lives in fear of any one who engages in this sort of act. I have studied the criminal mind for many years and there are certain traits that characterise a criminal. Over the last few days, I have tested Mr Yeats on each of these and each time he has come up as innocent. I assure you that he is an innocent. After all, my deduction that the perpetrator must be a small man, for only a man with a small hand could get the force from such a small handle as that found on these knives, left a possibility open; namely that the person we were looking for was not a man, but a woman. As soon as I saw the first clues, I should have realised; an occult activity, a ruthless mind and a small hand, I should have made the connection with Tanith Hekaltey, the Scarlet Woman who, I have to admit, outwitted me once before."

"So, if I get the story right, this whole set up is an occult activity that will, possibly, result in murder. Though the murder has not actually happened yet? What is Anna Giles's role in all this?" asked Lestrade, at pains in his ability to believe Sherlock Holmes's explanation of the case.

"I am not sure whether my theory about the centre of the pentagram is correct as of yet, Lestrade. Though you have to admit that the rest of my deductions have led us to advance our understanding."

"Yes, I'll give you that. So what is your next move? Are you going to drop the case in favour of my explanation, or are you going to continue with this silly theory about underground witches?"

Suddenly Holmes jumped from the chair and rushed past Lestrade towards the table. "That is it! That is it! She will not have the better of me this time," he cried continuously. He dragged the map from the table, spilling a pile of books in his haste to show us what he had thought out. "I know where the site of ritual is, for I am now certain that the ceremony has already happened."

"Then, where?" demanded Lestrade.

"We will not be able to do any more on it tonight, for I shall have to consult an acquaintance of mine as to how best we can get there."

"Yes, but where is it, Holmes?" I urged.

"Exactly where I predicted it to be, at the very centre of the pentagram."

"What? In the Whitechapel High Street?" I asked.

"Not in, Watson, under. Our opponent has carried out the ritual underground."

CHAPTER EIGHT
The Underground Tunnel

I retired to bed early that night, exhausted. When I arose the next morning, just after eight o'clock, it was obvious that Holmes had not been to bed at all. His face was drawn and the skin under his eyes had darkened; further, the front room of our apartment looked as if it had been turned over by a gang of thieves in the night.

"Ah, Watson, I apologise for the untidiness," said Holmes, "I have not had a very productive night, for all my efforts, but am awaiting a reply to the message I sent at first light. Hopefully that will take us someway further in our battle with the Scarlet Woman."

"Then your mind is made up that it is her?"

"Indeed it is, Watson. And how well she has done yet again, a most intelligent woman, but this time I am sure to win, for she has tripped up in giving us her identity and there will be a surplus of clues when we visit the site of ritual. For a start, I am sure we will soon know the whereabouts of Anna Giles."

The front door slammed beneath us and it seemed to make the whole house shake. Holmes did nothing except raise his eyes slightly toward me in an expression of anticipation. The door to our apartment opened without grace and a middle aged man hurried in, grappling with his flat cap, lest he should offend Holmes by either being late or forgetting to remove his headwear. The man was unshaven and his clothes were particularly soiled, so much so that it was necessary to open a window for fresh air. He did not give me a second glance, but looked down at Holmes who was watching him intently from behind his pipe. The man's rugged face cracked into a large smile, whereupon he opened a mouth without front teeth.

"Ah, Mr Kelly, you have made good time," said Holmes pleasantly, "This is my friend and colleague, Dr Watson."

"It is good to see you again, Mr Holmes, and I am very pleased to meet Dr Watson, perhaps if I could learn to read faster then I could enjoy Dr Watson's tales of your activities, and no mistake, but I am still in your debt for the help you gave to my dear wife. We have not forgotten you, Mr Holmes, and when your message came, she urged me not to keep you waiting."

"Then, Mrs Kelly is in good health?"

"Completely recovered, Mr Holmes, and no mistake. And, thanking you for your help – what can I do for you?"

"Good, then I hope you still work on the drains?"

"I do, Mr Holmes, though I have been in ill health because of it. But what other choice do I have? I will die underground before I get any other job."

"Would you explain to me where the tunnels go in the Whitechapel area and take us to a point that I shall show you. You have brought the plans?"

"I have brought the plans, Mr Holmes, but whatever you need, I would surely be the one to get it. The tunnels are no place for gentlemen such as yourselves."

"Nonsense, Kelly. You shall have some tea, perhaps some breakfast, and then you will show me these plans of yours."

It took some time to persuade Mr Kelly that he should take one of Mrs Hudson's breakfasts with us. I am sure he felt uncomfortable in what must have seemed to him luxurious surroundings, but he finally relented and sat down with us. I talked with him all the way through the meal, as I could see that Holmes had withdrawn into himself. Indeed, Holmes ate no more than three mouthfuls before he returned to his chair where he smoked his pipe. In the meantime, my conversation with Mr Kelly was as interesting as could be had with anyone. He worked as a tunneller, or so he called himself, by which his duties ranged from repairing tunnel walls to catching rats when they had become too numerous. His stories made me angry that someone could be made to work in such conditions when I did not laugh out loud at some of the queerer incidents that he recanted – the story of the alligator that had escaped from a pen on the dock and found its way into the London sewers was particularly fantastical. Mr Kelly would frequently break into bouts of heavy coughing, which made him embarrassed when he had managed to clear his breathing. I could diagnose his disease well enough, but I sensed that a name to that condition brought on by his continual exposure to methane was unlikely to be of interest to him.

"The plans, Mr Kelly, if you would be so good," said Holmes as we pushed our plates away from us.

Kelly arose and took himself out of the room, to where, no doubt, he had left his overcoat so he did not bring it in with him. He returned with sheets of decaying paper that looked as if they had spent as much time as he underground.

"There are no street names, Mr Holmes, for we go by what is underground not what lies above us," he explained apologetically, as he handed Holmes the papers.

"An easy enough problem to overcome, Mr Kelly," replied Holmes enthusiastically, "I have other maps that show where the entrances and exits to the tunnels are, so I can merely superimpose one map with the other." Holmes took his own maps from the basket next to the fire place. He looked for common points between the two maps and, on finding his references, placed the street map over Kelly's plans of the tunnels. In this way, he was producing a two dimensional replica of the layout of the Whitechapel area. He made numerous marks with a pencil, occasionally flicking the two maps away from each other, to ensure that he had the points exactly tallying. This was a cumbersome activity and, when he had made his rough calculations, he held the superimposed sheets to the light, so the marks came through unhindered. "I have it, Watson. There is indeed a labyrinth of tunnels running under Whitechapel High Street. We have the choice of three, by the look of it, so we shall need help. I shall telegraph Inspector Lestrade to come immediately and advise him to bring suitable clothes."

Without another word, Holmes left the room and fairly ran down the stairs. The excitement of the chase seemed to act on his nervous system in a way that no amount of stimulants ever could. I tried to resume my conversation with Mr Kelly, who was not over pleased by the prospect of accompanying a policeman through tunnels. I tried to draw him off this topic by enquiring as to how he knew Sherlock Holmes, but he would only reply enigmatically:

"He is a gentleman, and not too proud. Never a good man has walked these streets as has Mr Holmes. My wife owes him her life, and mine also. Such courage, who would have thought."

"It is settled," cried Holmes as he rushed back into the room, "Lestrade should be with us as soon as one of his horse-handling officers can be located. Now, Mr Kelly, we shall require to get to this point here." Holmes had taken up the plans once more and left his pipe to burn away of its own accord. He was pointing to where three sets of parallel lines interceded with each other. "I assume we can take this entrance here?"

"Not if you value your life you do not, Mr Holmes, that is the most dangerous spot in the whole of the city. It has caved in, you see, and, until the gas has been allowed to escape, we can go nowhere near it. We have blocked off all of the immediate holes from above ground. If you need to get to that part of the tunnel, we must go via the third tunnel here." Kelly had pointed to another spot on the map which was considerably further away from the intersection than the spot Holmes had originally asked about.

"You are invaluable, Mr Kelly, quite invaluable."

I looked over at Kelly, expecting to see some reaction but his face was expressionless. Holmes fell silent once more and rubbed his long chin with the tips of his fingers. Suddenly, he sat bolt upright. "Mr Kelly, when did this tunnel collapse?"

"Nigh on two weeks since. Killed five men, we have not even been able to recover the bodies. Most of the men refuse to go any where near the site, they have walked out rather than go down into the Whitechapel area. Indeed, the point you speak of under the High Street has not been checked since the tunnel caved in."

"Then tell me, if you would, the specifics of the collapse – is it not possible to go through it?"

"Certainly not, it has been blocked off completely. There is only one route to the intersection as I have shown you."

I was still pondering what use this information was when Lestrade came through the door. I had to look twice to see that it was indeed him. His clothing was a sight to behold. Away from the drab everyday garments we were used to seeing him in, he had seemed to amalgamate surplus garments of two different, minor regiments. The trousers looked very much as if they had seen the entirety of the Afghan campaign and, I fancy, had a stained knife cut in the lower leg. His jacket was that of a sergeant, for marks had been left where the stripes had been torn off. On his feet, he wore some heavy boots, that were not as worn as the rest of the clothing, so probably water tight – just right for a trip into the literal underworld of London.

"You have excelled yourself in your dress, Lestrade," said Holmes and even Mr Kelly had a slight smile on his face.

"Better to be prepared, Holmes," retorted Lestrade in good humour, "I even saw fit to bring yourself and Dr Watson a similar set of clothes." Holmes looked at him in horror as he emptied a large canvas bag onto the floor. There were indeed two sets of similar ex-army issue clothing. I bent towards them and picked out the two sets and offered them to Holmes to take his pick. He merely waved me away with the end of his pipe and so left me to choose. In the end my mind was made up, for only one was big enough to fit comfortably. I returned from my bedroom to a roar of laughter from Holmes.

I was annoyed. "You would be wise to take the other uniform, Holmes, you need protection against the rats, if nothing else."

"I am sure my old cloak will suffice, Watson, and my pair of stout walking boots."

As he had said, Holmes dressed himself in his usual style, albeit that they were older clothes, and so we were off, once again riding in the police carriage into the East End of London. It was Kelly who began to direct us once we had passed through the city and into the East End, though he seemed to do it more by looking at the direction of the roads than by the more familiar method of noting streets and their names. He had been quiet up until that point – in the way that men of his position would say nothing to a police officer for all the rewards it might lay at their feet.

The coach thundered on towards Whitechapel High Street. The snow had melted away from all the roads and only occasional icy remnants could be found. Holmes looked out keenly from his side of the carriage, his eyes lighting up spectacularly as he looked down upon the road when we eventually came to the five way junction that he had pin-pointed on the map as the place we were likely to find the body concealed. We took a sharp right, passing the beginning of Commercial Road, and turned into Leman Street, but had to pull into a smaller side street twice to make way for the trams that were coming up in the opposite direction. I heard the police driver complain about the huge monsters that were increasingly beginning to take up the road for themselves, only for him to be rebuked by Lestrade, who turned back into the cab and gave us a wink. Once we were on our way again, and the two trams were out of ear shot, it was possible to hear, and I fancy smell, the goods trains that had pulled in and out of the Gower Walk depot someway to our left. Holmes began to shuffle in his seat as we moved further and further away from the High Street. It was certainly going to be a long walk back up to the junction and all through underground tunnels.

"Turn in to the right here," ordered Kelly, in a meek voice that had to be relayed by the authority of Lestrade. The carriage pulled into Great Prescot Street and continued until we found ourselves amongst a plethora of small warehouses and depots, collectively known as Goodman's Yard. Kelly told Lestrade to stop the carriage and we alighted, leaving the driver to find a suitable place whereby he could leave the carriage and accompany us on Lestrade's orders. It cost Holmes a sovereign to arrange for a warehouse worker to take charge of the horse, after most people had shied away at the sight of a policeman; but, once the transaction was complete, Kelly called us over to a small yard, in the corner of which he was standing over a constructed box of wood that could not be more than a foot high. It was the outer trap door and it took the might of three of us to pull it from the position in which the cold weather had frozen it. Immediately, we were overcome by the stench of decay and Lestrade turned a pale shade, using his hand to cover both his nose and his mouth.

It only took Kelly on his own to lift the inner covering, increasing the stench to quite horrible proportions. He disappeared down the hole in the ground with his Davy lamp lit. I followed Holmes who had stepped into the hole with the eagerness of a blood hound on the trail of its target. Lestrade had thoughtfully lowered his lamp down into the hole so that I could see the rungs on the ladder that must have descended to at least thirty feet below the surface. Holmes and Kelly waited at the bottom of the ladder which ended in the middle of a tunnel that stretched into the darkness in both directions. The smell was almost intolerable and I could see in the dim light the brickwork that was built into a cylinder around us, damp with slimy small streams of liquid running from cracks. We all stood to the side of the floor, for a torrent of pungent liquid was running at some speed along the centre of the tunnel. On occasions it was possible to see the shape of a rat that had lost its footing being carried along by the current, helpless to change its direction until it reached the end of the stream.

It was indeed a gloomy prospect, having to travel up this tunnel, with bowed head, for the upper sides, where they curved over, could be no more than five feet from the floor. I had worked out roughly that to get all the way back to Whitechapel High Street, would be to travel in excess of a quarter of a mile. Once we were all assembled and Lestrade had berated his fellow officer for talk unbefitting of a man in uniform, we set off. Holmes had taken the lead, much to the apprehension of Kelly who was trying to keep up with the lamp. But Holmes was as sure of foot as if he had been brought up amongst the tunnels and did not stumble even when the rats came out in hordes, running over our feet and biting at the lower ends of our trousers. In places, the tunnel had fallen through and it was necessary to scramble across wet piles of rotting brick on hands and knees. It was in just such a case that a rat bit the hand of the police officer who, contrary to the shouts of Lestrade, ran back the way we had come, his screams echoing around the tunnel.

We must have been getting near to the interchange, for the tunnel widened and the rats were more numerous, seeming to pop out of every crack in the wall, including those in the ceiling above us. It was then that Holmes stopped and grabbed the lamp from Kelly. He bent over into the stream and studied the foul liquid intently. When he raised himself, there was an expression of confusion across his face, but he marched on without a word. Another hundred yards and we were at a point where another tunnel cut in from our left. Holmes marched on to his right, well before Kelly could give him the directions. Although the amount of water and rats running through the tunnel was now greater, the journey was more comfortable as the ceiling went high enough to clear all our heads. Holmes stopped again and tilted his head back as if looking at something he had spotted on the ceiling, but I realised that he was using his nose to detect a change in smell that, albeit very subtle, was definitely detectable once attention was drawn to it. It was not any more pleasant than the miasmatic stench of methane and other gasses, that I could tell.

"We are close, men, very close," muttered Holmes, more to himself but for the fact that his voice echoed loudly from all sides, above the gushing sound of the water and decaying matter that was lapping close to our feet. We stalked further forward, more slowly, towards the smell that was getting stronger with every step – the unmistakable smell of a dead, decaying body.

The tunnel grew wider and wider and somewhere in the distance, natural light was seeping through from above. I looked across at Kelly who had a certain look of foreboding at the light, it was a sign that the way ahead of us was indeed perilous. As we approached the source of light, which on closer inspection was no more than a thin slit in the ceiling where the mortar had been rotted away, it was possible to make out the junction of two tunnels and the one through which we were making our way. But it was not this that was taking Holme's attention, for there, immediately in front of us, darkened and barely recognisable was a form that could not be mistaken for anything other than a human corpse.

CHAPTER NINE
The Site Of Ritual

Holmes rushed through the final hazards of rats and fallen bricks to gain the first sight of his horrible discovery. As we increased our pace to catch up with him, I could see that he was waving his arms from side to side, to rid the body of the rats that were already devouring it. I have never seen such an abhorrent sight as that we were confronted with, for there, lying in a pool of water and effluent was a hunched figure, unrecognisable as the face had been eaten completely off by the rats. But there was no doubt of the cause of the death, for a dagger had been plunged into the heart and stuck out in all its repulsive glory, with a pentagram extending out from the end of the handle. There were a pile of clothes discarded at various points around the corpse and it was only from the style of the clothing that it was obvious the victim was a woman.

"I deduce that this is your missing prostitute, Lestrade," said Holmes calmly.

"It is the Ripper, back to haunt us again. There is no doubt about it, Holmes, the similarities are too much to leave to coincidence," cried Lestrade.

I have to admit at this point, as I looked down on the body of this poor woman, that I was inclined to agree with Inspector Lestrade for the similarities were definitely there. I looked to Holmes, but he was intently looking over the body in the greatest detail until he stood up straight and began to sift through the pile of clothes that were lying close by. Mr Kelly was leaning over the body with Lestrade, in much the same way as an inquisitive tourist looks over a picturesque waterfall. Kelly had obviously seen it all before, though the knife and the pentagram must have been unfamiliar to him.

"Mr Kelly, where is the tunnel in which the collapse has occurred?" said Holmes after some ten minutes of searching for clues, "I assume it to be this one." Holmes pointed across the junction into a tunnel that was smaller than the one we had come through.

"Yes, that's the one," replied Kelly.

"Good, because that is where the tracks lead," and before we could take in what Holmes had said, he headed off on his own. The shouts of protest from Kelly had no effect as Holmes disappeared into the darkness.

We were left on our own, standing under one of the busiest thoroughfares in London with a single lamp between us and suddenly it struck me that the temperature was considerably lower than it had been up in the streets. We all pulled our collars up and stood without sound, until the rats once again descended and we warmed ourselves in some little way by kicking out at them halfheartedly. I imagined what it would have been like to have come face to face with an alligator in one of these tunnels and rather than finding Kelly's earlier story humorous, I was filled with even more wonder at the man's everyday courage.

We heard his footsteps echoing all about us long before Holmes emerged from the tunnel opposite. He had a renewed urgency in every step he took and he almost bounded at Kelly, so much so that our guide took a step backwards into the stream of effluent, but did not seem to bat an eyelid at his precarious position.

"We must go at once, to the entrance which you say has been blocked off," said Holmes, "But above ground, not through the small gaps in there." He made some vague pointing motion to where he had ventured before turning on his heels and leading us back along the way we had come.

I have never been as grateful to breath London's infamous air than at the time we emerged from the underground tunnel into the corner of Goodman's Yard. Indeed, I fancy that my feelings were very much mirrored in the face of Lestrade who was extremely relieved at having come away from the expedition relatively unscathed. We were all drenched, not so much from the water falling on our heads from the cracks in the ceiling, but from the dampness that seemed to hang in mid-air throughout the tunnels.

We set off again, sheltering in the sides of the carriage that had been pulled up with some effort by the driver, trying to make a better impression on his superior. Kelly seemed to have taken heart from proving to all that he had the knowledge unequalled by any other man in London and began to issue directions between his frequent fits of coughing. We travelled northwards the way we had come and went straight across the High Street, up Commercial Street and right into Wentworth Street, where we were at once engulfed by crowds of children making their way from the school gates. I was surprised to see that when we eventually reached the school from where they were appearing, Kelly ordered us into the yard.

The entrance to the tunnels that had been boarded up was found in the corner of the school yard with various signs hanging off it, warning the children of the danger. Kelly led Holmes to it, while we lagged behind, the uniformed constable being crowded in by the children wanting to know what was happening. When we eventually reached the corner of the yard, and the constable was endeavouring to keep the children back, Kelly was saying to Holmes, "But I swear it was boarded up. I check that every three days, without fail. I assure you that none of the tunnellers would ever attempt to enter this way."

I looked over Holmes's shoulder as he was bent down, examining the pieces of timber that had been removed from the hole. Most of them were still in place though the nails that had been used to secure them were all missing or, rather, scattered about the floor.

"Then, if you are sure, Mr Kelly, this is a vital clue as to when this murder happened. Lestrade, it has occurred within the last two days, for Mr Kelly was due to check it tomorrow. What is more, it must have been done at night, for otherwise, the school would have noticed a woman climbing out."

"You are surely still not talking of a woman, Holmes? You should concede that you are wrong. There is no way that a woman could have navigated herself through those tunnels, while carrying her victim, just to dump the body before having the strength to make her way through piles of bricks from a cave-in and making good her exit through a boarded up hole."

"I can answer all those questions in turn, Lestrade. Firstly, there is no evidence whatsoever that the body was dumped in that tunnel. In fact, on the contrary, there are signs enough that the murder occurred at exactly the spot the body was found. If the murder had been committed above ground and the body dragged through the tunnel, the nature of that wound would have meant considerable blood loss. But you would have noticed that the rats were concentrated at one end of the tunnel in the main. If blood had dripped the length of the tunnel, then there should have been more rats feeding from the floor near to the entrance, where the loss of blood would have been at its most significant. So the victim was not carried, but rather went voluntarily – I shall explain the meaning of that later. Secondly, the holes I found made from where the collapse had occurred were dug out so that I would not have been able to fit. No man of average size would have been able to negotiate his way through that route."

"Ah, but you do not know that is the route that was taken."

"Elementary, I assure you. The slime on the floor of the tunnel revealed the single set of prints that led to, but not away from, the area that had collapsed. Compare that with the two sets of prints that were on the floor and in the same direction that we took. Hence I conclude that the two women made their way into the tunnel the way we had come in and then, once the murder was complete, the murderer made her way out through the area of collapse and through this exit here. I am afraid, Lestrade, that the facts speak quite plainly for themselves. The size of the single set of print is exactly that of the woman whom we suspect to be behind this queer case."

"Then, how on earth do you explain the strength needed to lift this boarded up exit from below?"

"Simple, the whole exercise was planned to the minutest detail. She visited this yard before going into the tunnel and, with the aid of a tool, no doubt, managed to remove the nails without any difficulty."

"Well, your explanation seems to fit the facts, Holmes, but I should very much think it a fantastical tale."

"Indeed it is that, Lestrade, but no more fantastical than the hearts that you yourself have observed. The whole thing has been set up so that the ritual can take place. Tanith Hekaltey has provided herself with a magical ring of protection, perhaps with the added advantage of throwing the police off her trail by linking it with Jack the Ripper, she has then made her sacrifice underground, where she will not be disturbed, and made good her escape through a tunnel that is not supposed to be negotiable."

"Then where do we start to look for her?"

"In a tobacco shop!" cried Holmes suddenly.

"How did you think of that?" I said.

"Well, Watson, take yourself back to when you came out of that tunnel. After taking a good few breaths of fresh air, what was the first thing that came to mind?"

"To have a cigarette," I conceded, "If only to get rid of that awful taste in my mouth."

"Exactly right. And look what we have here." Holmes bent down and picked up a half smoked cigarette.

We crowded around to observe his new discovery. "Well, there is no doubt that it is a woman we are looking for Holmes, there is lip rouge on the tip," I said quickly.

"I fear you may be mistaken, Watson, I am of the opinion that it is blood that has come from her lips. Though I should very much think it not to be of her own."

On hearing this, everyone gasped. Our singular case with the occult was becoming not only more bizarre, but much more disturbing with each new development. While we were all frozen in horror, however, Holmes had been turning the cigarette over and over in his hand and lifting it to his nose.

"You know it, Holmes?" I enquired.

"Watson, I doubt there is a tobacco I do not know. I have made a detailed study of some one hundred and ninety three different types of tobacco and the mixes that are associated with them."

"But I thought you had only reached as far as one hundred and forty eight," I said somewhat absently.

"Times do not stand still, Watson. If we are to keep ahead of the criminal element, it is necessary to acquaint ourselves with all new developments that come our way. But to answer the original question, I have no doubt that this will prove to be the one mistake that our Miss Hekaltey has made. It is a very poor tobacco, mainly consisting of that Dutch shag that only the destitute resort to. It is imported through one dock only and hence only a handful of shops in that district will stock it. It is certainly not from these parts, since the manufacturer of snuff and tobacco in the Minories is most popular. We shall need to travel further into the East End, to some of the roughest places known to the civilised world. We must be brave, for the docks in Poplar are not for the faint hearted and there are some men there who would pay handsomely to see me dead."

CHAPTER TEN
Poplar Docks

Against Sherlock Homes's wishes, Inspector Lestrade not only insisted on us taking the police carriage into Poplar, but also that he should accompany us. It was lucky for us that Mr Kelly explained to him just what would happen to a single policeman and his cab, if it was spotted in Poplar docks. Reluctantly, Lestrade accepted that discretion was the better part of valour and returned to Scotland Yard to organise the removal of Anna Giles's body from the drain in which it lay. Holmes assured him that we would report progress before we headed for Commercial Road and the tram that would take us into the heart of the docks. I must admit that the mode of travel in which we had engaged on our search eastwards over the last two days was becoming a firm favourite with me. There was no end of fascination in looking and studying the various types of people who used the tram system and even guessing at what their trade was. We were heading down Commercial Road, but the tram stopped little enough so it was in no time that we were on the East India Dock Road. I turned to Holmes as we passed close to the public house in which we had met the terrifying, but nevertheless very helpful, Mr Nailer.

"I assume that we are going to the East India Docks then, Holmes?" I said. I had visited the docks once before, when asked to attend to one of the sailors that had been struck with a most unusual tropical illness.

"Indeed we are, Watson, there is a small warehouse on the West Side of the dock that deals with all the imported tobacco from Holland. It is in this vicinity that the shops will sell this hard shag, for it is not even worth the cost of transporting it out of the warehouse. Normally it is only used by destitute seamen, not a tobacco I would immediately expect the young Tanith to be partial to. Though, that in itself is suggestive and I already have some theories as to where we might find her."

We did not speak for as long as it took to get to the West Side of the dock. Once away from the tram line, Holmes cut past the dock workers and headed straight for a small warehouse that looked as if it had been left derelict. The door was almost off its hinges and it creaked and groaned as Holmes pushed at it. I followed him into a small office that was empty but had a door set in its back wall which I assumed to lead straight to the warehouse itself. Holmes went straight for the door, seemingly uninhibited by what may lie behind it. The warehouse appeared to be almost empty, with little in it, apart from a single layer of tea chests in a far corner. Holmes gave a short gasp of exasperation and turned as if to leave, but in so doing attracted the attention of a small man who had gone unnoticed by me but had fallen into the trap Holmes had laid for him. He came bounding towards us, an angry look on his face.

"Oi! What's your business. This is private property, now tell me what you want or clear off."

I am sorry to disturb you, Sir," said Holmes calmly, 'We waited for some time in the office but nobody seemed to be around."

"Why did you not ring the bell, then?" The man almost yelled, keeping his body between ourselves and whatever business he had been conducting at the far end of the warehouse.

"I am so sorry, I did not see it, did you, Watson?'

"No, I must confess that I did not," I replied on cue.

"So, what's your business?"

"We know you are the sole importer of a rather harsh Dutch shag, I think it markets by the name of 'Cavalier'. We would like to purchase some for a friend and were wondering who you supplied it to."

"You want some Cavalier?" the man said, breaking into a laugh. "We can't give the stuff away, and no mistake. There is only one shop that will stock it and that is Robinson's across the way. But why don't you buy it from me? I could give you a whole chest full for what she will ask for an ounce."

"There is a specific mix I wish to be made up, but I thank you very much for your help." Holmes passed over a sovereign as he turned to leave and the man tipped his cap in appreciation.

When we were outside I asked innocently enough, what was the point of importing a tobacco that did not sell?

"Come now, Watson, you are not as innocent as all that, are you? Let me just say that tobacco is certainly less suspicious than sawdust and as such is most helpful in that age old trade of smuggling."

I was shocked that Holmes knew such things and took it upon myself not to ask him any more questions as we crossed the road away from the docks and walked past the Poplar Hospital. We walked perhaps another hundred yards before we came across the shop that had its name given to us. Inside this rather poorly lit emporium was an old oak table upon which was a set of scales. Behind the table, stacked untidily on the floor were crates of various sizes containing the different tobaccos. As soon as the door was shut, and the bell attached to the upper frame had rung out for the second time, a woman appeared through the rear door and moved herself behind the desk where she put her hands on her hips, and looked directly at us, challenging either myself or Holmes to make the first statement. As it was, Holmes was silent, surveying the inside of the shop for any clues.

"Well, Gentlemen, what may I do for you? You're not from around these parts are you? And I should not think that such gentlemen as yourselves would be interested in the tobacco I am selling." The woman said it not as a question, so much as a statement and held her head firm to prove that we were not going to outwit her.

"Ah, you are most astute, Madam, and as you have said, we are indeed not from around here. My name is Sherlock Holmes, and this is my friend Dr Watson."

Suddenly, there was a short yelp from the back room and a large mastiff ran into the shop. "Call it back, George, they are not the police!" yelled the woman as the dog flew past her. Holmes stood stock still, where he was, looking the dog straight in the eye just as it was about to jump for him. The dog yelped and sat on its back legs, looking up at Holmes with a cocked head.

A middle aged man came running after the dog, whistling for all his might. Even though the weather was probably still below freezing, the man wore a vest, and the braces that held his worn pair of trousers were flapping freely on the side of his legs. When he saw Holmes, and the large brute sat upright, he stopped and scratched his head in a puzzled way.

"Why, I have never seen such a thing," mumbled the man, as he swapped confused stares between his dog and Holmes. "Have you gone soft or something?" he yelled at the dog, who promptly turned around and growled fiercely at him. "You must be a magician," said the man good humouredly, "This dog frightens the life out of most folks. Whatever have you done to him?"

"I showed no fear, Sir, and a dog will not attack unless it can sense fear in a man. I believe most dogs are scavengers, living off scraps – unlike cats. If you had a lion in there I am sure I would not be standing here now."

"Why, then maybe I should get myself a lion," replied the man. The look of disbelief had gone from his face and he was smiling. "Now what is your business here? I was afraid you were the police."

"I feel most offended that we are seen all too often as the police, Watson," said Holmes to me.

"Well, in that case Sir, what did you say your name was?"

"Sherlock Holmes."

"Not the Sherlock Holmes? Why you must excuse us. I hope you have not brought that Inspector Lestrade with you?"

"Thankfully not, Sir, we are here to bring good news."

The woman remained in her position behind the table, making noises at her husband only to receive a short answer that, if they were not the police then they could call any time they should like.

"I am looking for a young woman – most beautiful – long hair. She has a northern accent. We have been searching for a day now and we do believe she buys her tobacco in this shop. We have some rather good news, which will be to her pecuniary advantage."

"Here isn't that your friend, Mabel?" said the man to his wife, who looked back at him with an evil, warning eye. Homes had picked up the look, but so had the man, "I thought so. Yes, the woman you are looking for does come in here."

"Then perhaps you would be so good as to tell us where we might find her, it is a fairly urgent matter."

"You had best ask my wife about that, Mr Holmes, she's the one that's filled up with all that superstitious nonsense. Maybe now we might be able to get rid of those bags, Mabel! You must excuse me, Sir, I have to be at work in half an hour."

The man left the front of the shop and disappeared back the way he had come, the large dog followed him with its tail between its legs. Holmes walked straight to the counter. "Then perhaps you could be of assistance."

The woman's resolute stance had been broken during the short conversation with her husband and she now looked upon Holmes with some nervousness.

"Please could you tell me where Miss Hekaltey is staying?" asked Holmes.

"I do not know, Sir," replied the woman quietly.

"Why, come now, your husband has just told us that you are well acquainted with her."

"We pass the time of day when she comes in, but I don't know anything else about the lady."

"Then please tell me what your husband meant when he talked of her bags," said Holmes firmly.

The woman shook suddenly and her head fell to her chest. "I have sworn that I should not speak to anybody of the matter, I have given my word."

"I am sure that Miss Hekaltey would be quite understanding when I give her the good news, she is due for a substantial amount of money, I assure you."

The woman gave Holmes a quick look, not at all sure of herself, nor whether to trust us. "She has left all her belongings with me until she leaves for America the day after next. Her bags are in the back of the shop."

"Then surely you know where she is staying?'

"I assure you, Mr Holmes, that I do not know."

"Very well, Madam, then I shall take up no more of your time. Thank you for your help." Holmes turned and grabbed me by the arm, leading me out of the door and into the cold air.

"Why, Holmes, should we not search the bags for a clue?" I asked once we had put some distance between ourselves and the shop.

"And arouse suspicion, Watson? I think not. If we searched her bags, you can be as sure that a message would have been got to her and then we would be as far as ever from finding her. Besides which, Miss Hekaltey has proved herself to be a cunning opponent: I doubt she would leave any clue in her baggage."

"Then we must have to wait for her to collect the bags?"

"Maybe, Watson, though her suspicions would definitely be aroused. She would rather forsake her belongings than come into contact with me. Anyway, I have a certain theory as to where we might find her."

"Please go on."

"All in good time, Watson, there is nothing that we can do for the next hour, so we shall warm ourselves with some of the local ale, to which I am quite partial."

Holmes led the way along the street and turned into an alley whereupon we found ourselves on the steps of a rather rough-looking public house. There could have been no mistaking the smell coming from the windows on the first floor either, the sickly scent of opium. I had reservations about entering such an establishment, but once inside realised that the opium rooms and the ale bars were separate. Holmes showed me to an empty table where, with my strange array of clothing, I was not given a second glance. The landlord talked as if himself and Holmes were old acquaintances, which they most probably were, before handing him two tankards of ale.

"There you are, Watson," said Holmes as he took his stool opposite me. "That should keep the chill away while we think over what our next move is to be."

"But you said that you knew where she was staying, Holmes, please tell me – I cannot stand the suspense."

"It is a relatively simple deduction really, Watson, I have merely combined two sources of information and deduced where she may be. First of all, there is the tobacco. No person would even contemplate smoking such harsh tobacco if they had the resources to purchase something slightly more refined. So we may take it as an assumption that she has very little money, most probably she has spent it all on the ticket to America we heard about. And it is likely to be a one way ticket, at that. Secondly, it is strange is it not, to leave all your belongings in the back of a shop in an area such as this, especially given that the shop owner, by which I take to be the man we have just seen, is obviously not well disposed to you. There is only one solution that fits these facts to my mind; that is that she is staying in a place where they will not let you have your own belongings."

"A prison?' I said.

"Nearly, a workhouse. There is the Poplar workhouse not far from here and I should think that we will find her among its residents."

CHAPTER ELEVEN
The Workhouse

We had one further drink before Holmes decided it was time to visit the work-house which, he assured me, was no more than five minutes walk from where we were. We made slow progress, however, for Holmes walked more slowly than was his wont and spoke little. When the huge, gloomy grey buildings were in sight he turned to me and said, "I think you had best have your revolver at the ready, Watson, for she is a desperate woman."

"How did you know I was carrying a revolver?"

"I saw you reach for it when you heard Mr Kelly's story of the alligators in the sewers. It was logical that you should bring it when you knew where we were heading."

"Quite irrational though," I said, embarrassed.

"Most irrational," smiled Holmes.

Rather than approach the obvious entrances at the front of the workhouse, Holmes cut down a side street, past a library building and towards the railway that was visible once we were behind the workhouse itself. We walked through one of the gates next to the line, whereupon Holmes turned and followed the single set of tracks that led up to the workhouse depot. We had not gone more than fifty yards before there was a voice from behind us, shouting for all its worth.

"Hey, get off those tracks, do you wanna be killed?"

"Indeed we do not," replied Holmes as he turned around to face the workman who had come running in our direction.

"You get back in the house, and take your friend with you if you know what's good for ya," growled the man at me.

"It is quite alright, Sir, we have not escaped and we are not inmates of the house," replied Holmes calmly, "But we are seeking a person who is. Indeed, if you are one of the depot's workers, you will know of her."

"I don't care for any of the scroungers we have in there, Sir, and mark my words, I wouldn't know any of that type." The man glared at the two of us. He was of stocky build, shorter than the average but was used to the rougher side of life. He only had three fingers on one of the hands he held clenched and ready by his side.

"Very well, if that is to be your tone, then I shall be forced to see your superior. If you would be as good as to point me in that direction."

"My superior? What's your business? I won't stand for things going above my head. I am the Foreman of this track and anything you want to discuss should go through me."

"Then perhaps you would be so good as to tell me where I might find Miss Hekaltey. A tall, long haired, most beautiful woman."

"I don't know what you are talking about," replied the Foreman, sullenly.

"Perhaps you have not heard the name but you know of whom I am speaking and are unwilling to cooperate. I have little option but to go to your superior."

"Now wait there, describe the woman and I may be able to help," said the man, in fear of Holmes's proposed course of action.

"Perhaps we might go inside, to discuss this. It would not do for us to be found out here, would it?"

The Foreman gave a shrug of his shoulders and led us along the railway track and into a large warehouse where the stench was almost more to stomach than the smell that still lingered in my nostrils from our trip through the tunnels. We walked past a short goods train that was being loaded with coffins. The Foreman shouted orders to some of his workmen who were wearing handkerchiefs over their noses and mouths, whilst they loaded this sad cargo.

"There has been an epidemic?" asked Holmes as we were led into a small room that was only large enough to offer three wooden chairs. At one end were charts, scribbled upon with pen, and a more official-looking timetable.

"Always is, at this time of year. Have to put extra men on to cope with the extra work," replied the man absently, "Shut the door, don't want the 'ole world to know."

I duly pushed the door as far as it would go before it stuck in its frame.

"A woman, beautiful, you must have noticed, quite tall..." began Holmes.

"Yes, I know who you mean," replied the man quickly, "What do you want with her?"

"It is most urgent, and personal. We need to speak with her and would be much obliged if you could fetch her for us. Please do not mention that she has visitors, but tell her there is a problem with some baggage she left in a shop and she should be the one to sort it out."

The man left without a word and I turned to Holmes for some explanation. He read my mind, as was usual, and replied, "It is not difficult to deduce, Watson. Our young Miss Hekaltey needs some way of getting in and out of the workhouse at will and that is only possible through this warehouse, all the other exits are strictly guarded, as I am sure you are aware. It is a rare occasion indeed that a person might leave this rather fearful establishment once they have been taken, unless of course we should count leaving on the back of that train we have just passed. It would not be a difficult feat for the charms and capabilities of Tanith to, by one way or another, influence the men who work here."

"It will be best now if we wait behind the door, for once she has seen us, she will not be disposed to remaining in our presence, we must cut her off from any escape route. Is your revolver ready?"

"Indeed it is, Holmes," I replied as we crouched behind the door that had been left open by the Foreman.

After little more than five minutes, the sound of a conversation growing nearer could be heard. It was the voice of the man who had just left us, explaining that someone needed to be talked to, lest their scheme was uncovered. We waited with bated breath to hear the reply, but there was none. The first we heard of Tanith Hekaltey was when she had walked into the centre of the room and spun around in surprise as we leapt out and blocked the door, leaving the Foreman banging from the outside.

"Mr Holmes! Another day and I should have escaped you for ever," she said calmly.

"Then you know exactly why we are here," replied Holmes.

"There could be many reasons, but I assure you that you shall never get the better of me."

I lifted the revolver even higher on hearing this and she replied with a mere smile.

"There are things you will never understand, Mr Holmes," she continued, "And I will never be caught where it really matters. You are in a dangerous position. You would be well advised not to interfere with forces of which you know so little."

"I do not believe in such things, Miss Hekaltey. Perhaps we should summon the police. The evil you have committed will lead you to the gallows." There was an obstinate silence, so Holmes continued, "Mr Crowley has left you, to go on to pastures new. He will not be back to help you, but will drop you the same as he has everyone else."

"You lie, Mr Holmes!" shrieked the woman, "He has his sacrifice and we are bonded together for all eternity, there is nothing that will come between us. I am the Scarlet Woman that rides upon the Beast, manifested away from my position as Mistress of the Masters of the Temple. I am the mystery of Babylon, the mother of abominations, and this is the mystery of her adulteries, for she hath yielded up herself to everything that liveth, and I have become a partaker in its mystery. And because I have made myself the servant of each, therefore I become the mystery of all!"

Holmes had hit the spot exactly, as the woman's face was now glowing with rage. She was shaking her long, untidy hair in anger and some of the strands stuck to the grime that had collected around her cheeks. If she were not to be taken to the gallows she would as likely end up in Bedlam.

"So, the poor woman you murdered was indeed no more than a rival for Crowley's attention – another believer in the occult, whom you could tempt into your underground chamber on the promise of some innocent act of supposed magic. But she was surely as attractive a proposition for Aleister Crowley as once you were."

The woman began to scream some indeterminate words and bent double with her hands to her ears, shaking herself violently. Holmes made for her and I followed. He grabbed one of her arms and I the other, though it took all my might to drag her upright. "You have taken a revenge on that woman who had replaced you

122

as Aleister Crowley's mistress, is that not so?" cried Holmes.

She immediately fell quiet and her body sagged as if all the life had left her. "You lie," she murmured, as she slipped into unconsciousness.

We carried her from the room and sat her out on a seat near to the small, remaining pile of coffins that were waiting to be loaded onto the train that had steamed up, waiting to depart. Holmes ordered me to take a look at her while he fought off the questions of the workhouse authorities who had been called by the Foreman. I heard him order a man to summon the police and for them to make haste in getting to us.

Tanith Hekaltey's face was placid, she lay unconscious as if she was merely asleep and experiencing a rather pleasant dream. She looked beautiful, her hair had been smoothed away from her face in the fall and it fanned across the stone floor. It was incredible that she could have been responsible for such an horrific crime.

She remained in a state of unconsciousness for the twenty minutes it took for Lestrade to reach the workhouse. He had been in Limehouse Police Station.

"Ah, Lestrade. Here is your killer," said Holmes.

"Then I shall get the handcuffs on her before you afford me some explanation," the Inspector replied, while he leaned toward her.

As he made to take her hand from the floor where it lay, she sprung into life and she caught Lestrade with her other arm, sending him off balance and into the side of a carriage of the train that had begun to pull away from the platform. While we were stunned by her sudden return to life, she leapt up and jumped at the handle on the end of the final carriage. She dragged herself up onto the pile of coffins and rolled over. Holmes grabbed the revolver from my hand and made to chase the quickly departing train, but he became entangled with Lestrade who was raising himself and the two of them tumbled to the floor. The train had left the small warehouse and was gaining some considerable speed. I picked the revolver from the floor, where it had fallen from Holmes's hand and took aim at the crouching figure on the last carriage. I fired twice, but was sure that both shots had missed. The woman had raised herself from her crouching position and was defiantly standing up, facing towards us as if inviting the bullet into her. But, before I could get another shot in, the train had lurched and she had lost her balance, falling from the back of the carriage onto the line.

Holmes bounded out of the warehouse and along the tracks, closely followed by myself and Lestrade. He bent down to examine the body but rose with a grave face as we caught up.

"Watson, if you please," Holmes said.

There was no pulse, nor did her eyes respond to light. "I think she has passed on, Holmes."

*　　*　　*

As we headed back towards the city, in the back of the police coach, the effect the culmination of this strange case had on us was evident. Holmes briefly explained the entirety of his deductions to Lestrade in such a detached way that it seemed far from a description of the events I had shared with him. Holmes even admitted his failings in the first meeting with the Scarlet Woman, the way she had managed to deceive him through great ingenuity and how she employed the same techniques as he would have. Leaving false trails had needed an understanding of Sherlock Holmes that was second to none. Perhaps, if it was not for the confidence Holmes put in Yeats, where many would have laughed at him, then the Scarlet Woman may have made her escape.

Lestrade was shaking his head slowly as Holmes fell silent. "Very, very strange. Very difficult to explain in a report."

"Indeed, Lestrade, very difficult. I never imagined Jack the Ripper to be so beautiful," replied Holmes with a sad smile.

GREENWICH EXCHANGE BOOKS

Student Guides

Greenwich Exchange Student Guides are critical studies of major or contemporary serious writers in English and selected European languages. The series is for the Student, the Teacher and the 'common reader' and are ideal resources for libraries. *The Times Educational Supplement (TES)* praised these books saying "The style of these guides has a pressure of meaning behind it. Students should learn from that .... If art is about selection, perception and taste, then this is it."

(ISBN prefix 1-871551- applies)
The series includes:
W. H. Auden by Stephen Wade (-36-6)
William Blake by Peter Davies (-27-7)
The Bröntes by Peter Davies (-24-2)
Joseph Conrad by Martin Seymour-Smith (-18-8)
William Cowper by Michael Thorn (-25-0)
Charles Dickens by Robert Giddings (-26-9)
John Donne by Sean Haldane (-23-4)
Thomas Hardy by Sean Haldane (-35-1)
Seamus Heaney by Peter Davies (-37-8)
Philip Larkin by Warren Hope (-35-8)
Shakespeare's Poetry by Martin Seymour-Smith (-22-6)
Tobias Smollett by Robert Giddings (-21-8)
Alfred Lord Tennyson by Michael Thorn (-20-X)
W.B. Yeats by Warren Hope (-34-X)

Other titles planned include:
20th Century: T. S. Eliot; Ford Madox Ford; Robert Graves; Dylan Thomas
19th Century: Arnold; Jane Austen; Browning; Byron; John Clare;
S. T. Coleridge; George Eliot; John Keats; Oscar Wilde; Wordsworth
18th Century: Fielding, Dr Johnson; Alexander Pope; Richardson;
Laurence Sterne; Sheridan; Dean Swift
17th Century: Congreve; Dryden; Ben Jonson; Marlowe; Milton; Rochester

Early writings: Chaucer; Skelton

European Languages
Fifty European Novels by Martin Seymour-Smith (-49-8)

French Authors
Balzac by Wendy Mercer (-48-X)

Other titles planned include:
Apollinaire; Céline; Gide; Proust; Rimbaud; Tournier, Verlaine; Zola

German Authors
Goethe; Heine; Thomas Mann; Rilke

OTHER GREENWICH EXCHANGE BOOKS

All paperbacks unless otherwise stated.

LITERATURE & BIOGRAPHY

"The Author, the Book & the Reader" *by Robert Giddings*
This collection of Essays analyses the effects of changing technology and the attendant commercial pressures on literary styles and subject matter. Authors covered include Dickens; Smollett; Mark Twain; Dr Johnson; John Le Carré.
ISBN 1-871551-01-0 Size A5 approx; 220pp; illus.

"In Pursuit of Lewis Carroll" *by Raphael Shaberman*
Sherlock Holmes and the author uncover new evidence in their investigations into the mysterious life and writing of Lewis Carroll. They examine published works by Carroll that have been overlooked by previous commentators. A newly discovered poem, almost certainly by Carroll, is published here. Amongst many aspects of Carroll's highly complex personality, this book explores his relationship with his parents, numerous child friends, and the formidable Mrs Liddell, mother of the immortal Alice.
ISBN 1-871551-13-7 Size 70% A4; 130pp; illus.

"Norman Cameron" *by Warren Hope*
Cameron's poetry was admired by Auden; celebrated by Dylan Thomas; valued by Robert Graves. He was described by Martin Seymour-Smith as one of "... the most rewarding and pure poets of his generation..." is at last given a full length biography. This eminently sociable man, who had periods of darkness and despair, wrote little poetry by comparison with others of his time, but always of a high and consistent quality - imaginative and profound.
ISBN 1-871551-05-6 A5 size; 250pp; illus.

"The Essential Baudelaire" *by Professor F. W. Leakey*
A chronological survey of Baudelaire's writings this book will offer for the first time in Baudelaire studies, a comprehensive survey of his writings in their full chronological development. Baudelaire's development is explored under five headings: the Verse Poet; the Novelist in Miniature; the prose Poet; the Critic and Aesthetician; the Moralist; the translator. This book will interest Baudelaire specialists as well as the general reader.
ISBN 1-871551-3 A5 size; 300pp; illus.

"'Liar! Liar!': Jack Kerouac–Novelist" *by R. J. Ellis*
The fullest study of Jack Kerouac's fiction to date. It is the first book to devote an individual chapter to each and every one of his novels. *On the Road, Visions of Cody* and *The Subterraneans*, Kerouac's central masterpieces, are re-read in-depth, in a new and exciting way. The books Kerouac himself saw as major elements of his spontaneous 'bop' odyssey, *Visions of Gerard* and *Doctor Sax*, are also strikingly re-interpreted, as are other, daringly innovative writings, like 'The Railroad Earth' and his 'try at a spontaneous *Finnegans Wake'*, *Old Angel Midnight*. Undeservedly neglected writings, such as *Tristessa* and *Big Sur*, are also analysed, alongside better known novels like *Dharma Bums* and *Desolation Angels*.

Liar! Liar! takes its title for the words of *Tristessa's* narrator, Jack, referring to himself. He also warns us 'I guess, I'm a liar, watch out!'. R. J. Ellis' study provocatively proposes that we need to take this warning seriously and, rather than reading Kerouac's novels simply as fictional versions of his life, focus just as much on the way the novels stand as variations on a series of ambiguously-represented themes: explorations of class, sexual identity, the French-Canadian Catholic confessional, and addiction in its hydra-headed modern forms. Ellis shows how Kerouac's deep anxieties in each of these arenas makes him an incisive commentator on his uncertain times and a bitingly honest self-critic, constantly attacking his narrators' 'vanities'.

R. J. Ellis is Professor of English and American Studies at the Nottingham Trent University. His commentaries on Beat writing have been frequently published, and his most recent book, a full modern edition of Harriet Wilson's *Our Nig*, the first ever novel by an African American woman, has been widely acclaimed.
ISBN 1-871551-53-6 A5 size; 300pp

PHILOSOPHY

"Marx: Justice and Dialectic" *by James Daly*
Department of Scholastic Philosophy, Queens University, Belfast.
James Daly shows the humane basis of Marx's thinking, rather than the imposed "economic materialistic" views of many modern commentators. In particular he refutes the notion that for Marx, justice relates simply to the state of development of society at a particular time. Marx's views about justice and human relationships belong to the continuing traditions of moral thought in Europe.
ISBN 1-871551-28-5 A5 size; 180 pp

"Whitehead's Philosophy" *by Dr T. E. Burke*
Department of Philosophy, University of Reading
Dr Burke explores the main achievements of this philosopher, better known in the U.S. than Britain. Whitehead, often remembered as Russell's tutor and collaborator on *Principia Mathematica,* was one of the few who had a grasp of relativity and its possible implications. His philosophical writings reflect his profound knowledge of mathematics and science. He was responsible for initiating process theology.
ISBN 1-871551-29-3 A5 size; 180pp

POETRY

"Wilderness" *by Martin Seymour-Smith*
This is Seymour-Smith's first publication of his poetry for more than 20 years. This collection of 36 poems is a fearless account of an inner life of love, frustration, guilt, laughter and the celebration of others. Best known to the general public as the author of the controversial and best selling *Hardy* (1994).
ISBN 1-871551-08-0 A5 size; 64pp

Baudelaire: "Les Fleurs du Mal in English Verse" *translated by Professor F. W. Leakey*
Selected poems from *Les Fleurs du Mal* are translated with parallel French texts, are designed to be read with pleasure by readers who have no French, as well as those practised in the French language.

F. W. Leakey is Emeritus Professor of French in the University of London. As a scholar, critic and teacher he has specialised in the work of Baudelaire for 50 years. He has published a number of books on Baudelaire.
ISBN 1-871551-10-2 A5 size 140pp

"Shakespeare's Sonnets" *edited by Martin Seymour-Smith*
This scholarly edition follows the original text of the 1609 Quarto - which, with newly revised notes and introduction by Seymour-Smith – provides an insight with which to judge Shakespeare's artistic intentions.
ISBN 1-871551-38-2 A5 size; 120pp

THEATRE

"Music Hall Warriors: A history of the Variety Artistes Federation" *by Peter Honri*
This is an unique and fascinating history of how vaudeville artistes formed the first effective actor's trade union in 1906 and then battled with the powerful owners of music halls to obtain fairer contracts. The story continues with the VAF dealing with performing rights, radio, and the advent of television. Peter Honri is the fourth generation of a vaudeville family. The book has a foreword by the Right Honourable John Major MP when he was Prime Minister – his father was a founder member of the VAF.
ISBN 1-871551-06-4 A4 size; 140pp; illus.

SHOESTRING PRESS BOOKS

"Raising Spirits, Making Gold & Swapping Wives: The True Adventures of Dr John Dee & Sir Edward Kelly" *by Michael Wilding*

In London in 1583 the mathematician John Dee and the seer Edward Kelly began summoning up a succession of spirits, who instructed them in the secrets of the universe and warned them of imminent apocalyptic change. Attaching themselves to the visiting Polish Count Laski, they set off for Europe, taking with them a mysterious alchemical elixir discovered in the Cotswolds. Queen Elizabeth summoned them back to England to share their alchemical expertise and sent the poet Edward Dyer to collect them.

The surviving confidential reports, letters, diaries and secret spiritual records are assembled there into a compelling narrative, all the more amazing for being truer than any fiction.

Michael Wilding is one of Australia's most distinguished writers. *The New York Times Book Review* said of him, "He's so good that you're willing to forgive him anything." He has published numerous novels and collections of short stories as well as studies of Milton, on whom he is an acknowledged expert, and such ground-breaking critical works as *Social Vision* and *Studies in Classic Australian Fiction.*

"Goodbye Buenos Aires" *by Andrew Graham-Yooll*

Buenos Aires in the 1920s and 1930s was a fascinating destination for a young person looking for a new life, a place of fantasy, adventure and prospects of fast wealth. This is the city which the author's father discovered for himself in October, 1928, when he arrived there, penniless from Edinburgh.

This book is at once a memoire of separation, of the harsh reality of unpredictable politics of personal loss, and of love rediscovered.

Andrew Graham-Yooll, who was born in Buenos Aires in 1944, is a journalist on the *Buenos Aires Herald.* He formerly worked for *The Daily Telegraph*, and was the editor of *Index on Censorship.* Among his many books are *A State of Fear*, and *The Forgotten Colony: A History of the English-Speaking People in Argentina.*